Can this lady really teach ballet?

"The class was supposed to start half an hour ago, Mom," Charlie said as they stood outside of Miss Claudine's School of Ballet. "Can't we just go home? It doesn't look like the teacher's going to show up."

"I don't know, Charlie," Mrs. Clark insisted. "I think we should stay a few minutes and see what happens."

Just then Charlie turned and saw a woman come hurrying toward them. She was tall, thin, and wore a lavender leotard over which she'd wrapped a calf-length dance skirt of the same color. Her skin was pale, and her nose and chin somewhat pointy, but her blue eyes seemed to shine. As she approached she pulled off her red hat, sending her long ash-blond hair swirling around her shoulders.

"Pardonnez-moi, mesdemoiselles!" the woman cried as she neared the group waiting around the locked door of the studio. *"Pardonnez-moi!"* Whipping a ring of clattering keys from her large black pocketbook, she unlocked the door and flung it open dramatically. *"Voila!"* she exclaimed.

"Do you think that's Miss Claudine herself?" Charlie asked her mother in disbelief. "She looks like some kind of a nut to me."

No Way Ballet

STEPPING OUT

by Suzanne Weyn

Illustrated by Joel Iskowitz

Troll Associates

Library of Congress Cataloging-in-Publication Data

Weyn, Suzanne.
    Stepping out / by Suzanne Weyn; illustrated by Joel Iskowitz.
      p.   cm.—(No way ballet ; #1)
    Summary: Three girls become friends when they skip ballet class
and spend a calamity-filled afternoon in a shopping mall.
   ISBN 0-8167-1619-6 (lib. bdg.)   ISBN 0-8167-1620-X (pbk.)
   [1. Ballet dancing—Fiction. 2. Friendship—Fiction.]
I. Iskowitz, Joel, ill. II. Title. III. Series: Weyn, Suzanne. No
way ballet ; #1.
PZ7.W539St 1990
[Fic]—dc19   89-30586

A TROLL BOOK, published by Troll Associates,
Mahwah, NJ 07430

Printed in the United States of America.

10 9 8 7 6 5 4 3 2 1

One

Charlie Clark stretched out luxuriously on the living-room sofa. This was heaven. Friday afternoon and no one was home. Her mother was at the mall, her father still at work, and her three brothers all at football practice. With the remote control in her hand, Charlie had complete control of the television. She was queen of the airwaves with no one to disturb her.

Click. Charlie checked in to see how Reva Harris was doing on *Search for Love,* her favorite soap opera. Charlie admired Reva. When she watched the beautiful actress toss her silky black hair over her shoulders and say something witty, Charlie would toss her fine, straight hair and repeat the words Reva said. Somehow they sounded better when Reva said them. It was hard for a ten-year-old girl to sound convincing saying things like, "I've been truly in love with all the men in my life." Still, Charlie liked to dream she was a tall, raven-haired beauty, instead of a short, red-haired fifth-grader.

When *Search* had a commercial break, Charlie clicked the remote to watch the game show *Prize Bonanza.* "Go for car number three!" she cried, enjoying the way her voice mixed with that of the screaming studio audience. "The magic key is in the backseat of the Horizon." But no, the contestant went for the Mustang

1

convertible and lost. Sure enough, the magic key was in the Horizon. "I've just got to get on that show," Charlie muttered, imagining herself behind the wheel of a gleaming new car, waving happily to the audience.

Charlie heard the jangle of keys in the front door and quickly switched to the educational channel. *Cooking Around the World* was on. A man in a white chef's hat was demonstrating how to wrap a hen in pastry dough. Charlie sat up straight and rested her chin on the palm of her hand, trying to look completely absorbed in the program.

Charlie's mother stepped into the living room, her arms loaded with packages. She looked at her daughter and sighed. "It's a gorgeous day, Charlie," she said. "The sun is shining, the leaves are starting to turn color. Why don't you go outside and enjoy it?"

"But, Mom, I'm watching educational TV. See," Charlie protested, pointing to the screen.

Mrs. Clark laughed despite herself. "I'm sure knowing how to wrap a Cornish hen in pastry dough will come in very handy someday," she said.

"You never know, Mom," Charlie said seriously, not taking her eyes from the set.

Mrs. Clark settled on the edge of the big plaid couch and watched the program for a few minutes. "Did they ever find Reva's half-brother?" she asked casually.

Charlie's eyes lit with enthusiasm. "Just today they discovered that Reva's demented twin sister, Alice, kidnapped . . ." Charlie cut herself short. "That's no fair, Mom."

"Caught you," her mother teased, poking Charlie in the shoulder. "I'm sorry, Charlie, but I can't stand to

2

see my darling daughter turning into a couch potato before my very eyes."

"There's nothing else to do since Karen moved," Charlie argued. Karen was Charlie's best friend. This past summer, Karen had moved to Chicago when her father had been transferred.

"All you and Karen used to do was watch TV together," Mrs. Clark pointed out.

"That's why we were such good friends. Karen really knew how to have fun. She could tune in channels we don't even get."

"I remember. We were all watching Spanish-speaking stations for two days until she came over and readjusted the set."

"She's really talented," Charlie said fondly.

"Yes, well . . . I think it's time you thought about developing some talents of your own," Mrs. Clark said as she rose from the couch and hung her car coat in the front hall closet. Charlie didn't like the look on her mother's face. There was a certain twinkle in her blue eyes that Mrs. Clark got when she was in the grip of some great new idea. Her mother's "great ideas" always involved moving Charlie off the big, comfortable couch and away from the television set and into some activity that Charlie inevitably despised.

"I have lots of talents, Mom," Charlie insisted, knowing that she would have to think and talk fast. "I'm good at . . . English in school, and . . . I was second runner-up in an essay contest last year. My essay was called 'TV, the World's Greatest Invention,' remember?"

Charlie's mother chuckled and settled into the big, gray overstuffed chair next to the couch. "Yes, you were

very convincing. I even remember the last line: 'If the great light of TV is ever turned off, our world will fall into a horrible darkness.' "

Charlie was glad her mother remembered that line since she was still very proud of it. She tried to think of some more talents she possessed. *I can play the themes from six different sitcoms on the phone touch-tones,* she thought, but then decided that might backfire with her mother. She could list every new car that had been advertised on TV in the last three months. But no, her mother wouldn't be impressed.

"I know you're talented," Mrs. Clark said. "That's exactly why I don't want to see you wasting your potential by sitting in front of the TV."

"You learn a lot of interesting things on TV," Charlie protested. "You learn all about how criminals think, and how the police catch them. You get to see how people who are rich and famous live. I mean, can you really think of a better way for me to spend my time?" Charlie winced; she knew that last sentence had been a mistake. Her mother could *always* think of a better way for her to spend her time. Better in her mother's eyes, anyway.

"What do you think of ballet?" Mrs. Clark asked, too casually. Her tone of voice put Charlie on the alert. There was no mistaking it: Mrs. Clark had just come up with another of her "great ideas."

"There's a perfect example," said Charlie in one last desperate attempt to sidetrack her mother. "Educational TV has some great ballets coming up. I hadn't planned to watch them, but if you'd like me to—no problem."

"I was thinking more along the lines of *learning* ballet," her mother said. "I think you'd be terrific at it."

There it was. The "great idea" was out. And it was even more horrible than Charlie had expected. "Ballet?" she shrieked. "Ballet! Mom, you know I'm totally uncoordinated. I practically failed gym last year."

"That's all the more reason for you to take ballet lessons," her mother insisted as she leaned forward in her chair. "Besides, everyone in this family is athletic. You're just out of shape because you spend every minute glued to the tube."

"But, Mom . . . but, but," Charlie stammered, jumping to her feet. "It's really not a good time for me. You've been bugging me to clean my room, and I was planning to do it this Saturday—and who knows how long that's going to take. It could take days . . . months. And I have to do a science project for school, and I . . . and I . . ."

"Your room can wait," her mother said. "I'd rather see you take the ballet lessons. I'm sure you'll get your science project done, too."

Charlie looked pained. "Do I have to, Mom?"

"I'm going to insist that you at least give it a try. I noticed a cute-looking ballet school today when I was at the Eastbridge Mall, Miss Claudine's School of Ballet. Here." Mrs. Clark reached into her pocket and unfolded a pink piece of paper. "I went in and got a schedule of beginner classes. They've just started. You'll only have missed three or four classes."

Cute! Charlie thought with disbelief. How could any school be cute? This was awful. It was bad enough that she had to suffer through gym twice a week. Now she was going to have to suffer through ballet classes, too! It was just one more embarrassing opportunity for her

6

to demonstrate to the world that she was totally, hopelessly uncoordinated.

"But I won't know anybody there," Charlie whined, feeling as if her world was coming to an end.

Mrs. Clark looked thoughtful. "You've just given me a great idea," she said. "At the last PTA meeting some of the parents were looking for activities to involve their children in. I'm going to call the parents on my PTA list and see if there are any who'd like to enroll their kids in ballet class. Maybe we could even car-pool it. This is going to work out perfectly."

Charlie plopped face down onto the couch and moaned loudly into the cushions. It kept getting worse and worse. Now that she thought of it, she didn't want anyone she knew to be in her ballet class. Now all the kids at school would hear how klutzy she was in ballet. She could just imagine them calling her "Twinkle Toes Clark" and giggling as she walked down the hall.

"Don't be so melodramatic, Charlie," her mother said. "I think you'll really like ballet. I'm going to make those calls right now. If I can get this organized, we can start you tomorrow in a Saturday beginners' class."

Charlie lifted her head. "Tomorrow!" she wailed. "Isn't that a little sudden?"

"Why wait?" her mother asked cheerily. She gathered her packages and went upstairs humming a tune from *The Nutcracker* ballet.

Charlie rolled over on the couch and clicked the remote control back to *Search for Love.* Reva Harris had failed to rescue her half-brother and was talking to her boyfriend at a cafe near the ocean. Her long hair was blown back by the breeze as she looked straight into the camera. "Some days start out so well," she said, "and then—*poof*—disaster strikes."

"You can say that again, Reva," Charlie muttered. "You can sure say that again."

At eight-thirty the next morning, Mrs. Clark peeked into Charlie's bedroom. "Let's go, Charlie. We have to be at Miss Claudine's by ten-thirty to register before class, and I have to pick up Emma and Lindsey along the way."

Charlie pulled the covers over her head. "This isn't happening. It's all a dream," she mumbled to herself hopefully. Charlie couldn't believe that her mother had actually convinced Lindsey Munson's father to make his daughter take ballet. Lindsey was in Charlie's class, but they didn't hang around with the same kids. The thing that impressed Charlie most about Lindsey was that Lindsey was actually shorter than she was. Other than lack of height, they had nothing in common. Lindsey was the kind of girl who seemed more like a boy to Charlie. All Lindsey lived for was playing sports, while Charlie devoted a great deal of time to avoiding physical activity of any kind, so it wasn't strange that the two girls didn't have much to say to each other. Nonetheless, Charlie could not picture square-shouldered, boyish Lindsey in a ballet class.

The other girl who had been ensnared in the web of Mrs. Clark's "great idea" was Emma Guthrie. Emma was new in school, so Charlie didn't know anything about her—except that she struck Charlie as sort of strange. She liked to dress in black and purple and sometimes wore lipstick and mascara to class. No one else in the fifth grade at Eastbridge Elementary wore

8

makeup, and Charlie couldn't think of anyone besides Emma who wore purple and black. Charlie wasn't sure whether Emma was the ballet type or not. It was possible that she was.

"Come on, Charlie," her mother called up the stairs.

Charlie rolled out of bed and went to the top of the stairs. "I don't have any ballet stuff to wear. I can't go."

"It says on the schedule that leotards are provided. Just wear something comfortable."

It was clear to Charlie that there was no getting out of this, so she pulled on her jeans, her big, nubby blue knit sweater, and her new pink high-top sneakers and headed downstairs.

"It's the ballerina!" shouted Charlie's thirteen-year-old brother Harry when she was halfway down the stairs. Harry and John, her fifteen-year-old brother, were sitting on the couch watching TV. Even though they were a year and a half apart, everyone always said John and Harry could be twins. They both had the same wavy, reddish-brown hair, freckles, and the same hazel-colored eyes. This year, though, John had grown to be just under six feet, which made him about four inches taller than Harry.

When they saw Charlie they leaped to their feet and began spinning around the living room on their toes with their arms held over their heads. The sight of these big spinning hulks might have made Charlie laugh on another day, but today she didn't appreciate the joke.

Charlie stuck her tongue out at them and proceeded down the stairs. Her two brothers weren't about to let her pass so easily. They came up behind her, and each boy grabbed hold of her from under her armpits and lifted her into the air.

"Hey, cut it out!" she shouted, swinging her legs wildly, trying to kick her brothers. Laughing and still doing their comical imitation of ballet dancers, Harry and John carried her into the kitchen.

"That's enough," scolded Mrs. Clark, who was sitting at the kitchen table with Mr. Clark and Charlie's oldest brother, Frank. "Sit down and eat these eggs before they get cold."

Charlie pushed her eggs around on her plate as her brothers talked about the big varsity football game coming up between Eastbridge High and Highland Park High. Seventeen-year-old Frank was the captain of the varsity football team, and John was on the team, too. Harry wasn't playing because he was on the junior varsity team, but he was just as excited about the game as his brothers were.

"We're going to cream 'em. Cream 'em," Frank was explaining. Charlie rolled her eyes. She would never understand what the big deal was about running up and down a field holding a ball and trying not to get mowed down by other big guys in football gear. It sounded to Charlie more like a punishment than something you'd actually do for fun.

Charlie looked at her father, who was sitting next to Frank. She decided that Harry, John, and she looked like their father. Frank, with his blue eyes and dark brown hair, looked more like their mother. One thing they all had in common though was that they were tall. Charlie couldn't figure how she'd turned out to be such a runt in this family of giants. Her mother said she wasn't done growing yet, but, still, she was one of the shortest kids in her class.

"So, you're off to a new adventure this morning, I

hear," her father said pleasantly, turning away from the football conversation and toward Charlie.

"Please, I was trying not to think about it," Charlie answered grimly. She knew there was no sense in begging her father to let her stay home. Her parents always stuck together on decisions like this.

"Ah, come on," he coaxed, "it'll be fun."

"Yeah, some fun," Charlie muttered, still pushing her scrambled eggs around on her plate. She didn't feel like eating. Maybe she could say she'd lost her appetite because she was sick. No, she'd tried that just last week when she wanted to stay home to avoid a physical-fitness test at school. Her parents hadn't fallen for it then—and they hadn't even known about the test. Today they'd be on the lookout for any tricks like that.

"Come on, Charlie, we'll be late," her mother said all too soon.

"Ta ta," Harry teased in a silly high-pitched voice, waving his napkin at Charlie.

"You'll do great, squirt," Frank said kindly.

"Yeah, sure," Charlie mumbled, as she pushed her chair out from the table. "And don't call me squirt."

"Knock 'em dead," called her father.

Charlie followed her mother outside and slid into the front seat of the family's blue hatchback. "Let's see now," said Mrs. Clark as she and Charlie fastened their seat belts. "Emma Guthrie lives on Maplewood, number seventy-six. I guess we should pick her up first."

Charlie decided to try one last strategy. "You know, Mom, Emma Guthrie is kind of weird. I'm not sure you want me hanging out with her."

"Her mother sounded perfectly nice on the phone. What's weird about Emma?"

"I can't explain it. You'll see," Charlie said, folding her arms and resigning herself to her horrible fate. Up until now ballet class had seemed the worst of her troubles. Suddenly she felt shy and uncomfortable at the thought of having two girls whom she wouldn't ordinarily have anything to do with sitting right there in her family's car.

Mrs. Clark turned the car through the tree-lined streets of Eastbridge until they came to Maplewood. She pulled into the driveway of a small cedar-shingled house. Immediately the front door of the house opened, and a petite woman with dark, almost black hair pulled back tightly into a braid waved at them. She disappeared back inside the house and didn't return.

"I wonder what's going on," Mrs. Clark said, looking at her watch.

"I told you she was weird," said Charlie matter-of-factly.

The door flew open again, and Charlie and her mother heard the sound of raised voices coming from the house. "You're going and that's final!" Mrs. Guthrie shouted.

A moment later Emma appeared on the front steps wearing a purple quilted jacket and black stretch pants. Her long brown hair was pinned up on one side with a bright red plastic clip. Her mother quickly stepped out next to her. Emma glowered at her mother with defiant eyes as Mrs. Guthrie took hold of Emma's arm and guided her sternly toward the car.

Charlie looked at her mother to gauge her reaction to the scene. Just as she'd hoped, her mother's brows were knit, and her lips had tightened into a look of anxious disapproval.

When they were just a few feet from the car, Emma suddenly balked and started pulling away. But Mrs. Guthrie had her in an iron grip. No matter how hard Emma pulled, she couldn't escape.

"See what I mean," Charlie pressed, hoping against hope that her mother would be so appalled by Emma's behavior that she'd decide she didn't want Charlie influenced by the girl. "Weird."

"Hmm," her mother nodded absently.

Mrs. Guthrie now held Emma's two arms firmly. They were near enough to the car that Charlie could hear what she was saying.

"Look, Emma, you have everything it takes to be a great dancer," Mrs. Guthrie said in a low, angry voice. "I don't know why you're being so obstinate about this."

"I don't want to be a dancer, I want to be a painter," Emma shouted.

"How do you know what you want to be? You're only ten years old," Mrs. Guthrie snapped. "Besides, you're making a scene in front of these people."

Her mother's last words seemed to make an impression on Emma. She looked over to the car quickly. With an air of wounded pride she straightened her shoulders and said, "All right, Mother, since you don't care how I feel, I suppose I'll have to go." Tossing her head back like a princess who was suffering a great injustice, she walked toward the car.

Charlie certainly understood how Emma felt, even though she couldn't picture herself behaving like Emma in a million years. Charlie knew her mother would tolerate her acting up like that for about two minutes, and then she'd be sent to her room for at least the rest of

13

the day. But, with a sigh, Charlie realized her mother wasn't horrified enough by Emma to forget about ballet.

Emma sat down in the backseat of the car. "Hello, Emma," said Mrs. Clark brightly. "I think you know Charlie from school, and I'm Mrs. Clark."

"Pleased to meet you," Emma said with flat primness, not even bothering to acknowledge Charlie's presence.

"I'm sure you'll both really like this class once you get started," Charlie's mother chirped happily.

"I don't think so," said Emma. "I've taken ballet classes before and I've detested every moment."

Charlie slumped down in her seat and jammed her hands in her jeans pockets. This was going to be a long day.

Two

"I can't believe this!" cried Mrs. Clark, sticking her head out the car window to survey the traffic tie-up ahead of her. "If they don't move that stalled car soon, we'll be late."

"No problem, Mom, really," said Charlie.

"We don't mind at all, honestly," insisted Lindsey Munson from the backseat. They'd picked up Lindsey after Emma. Though she didn't throw a tantrum, as Emma had, it was clear from her grim attitude that she was no more thrilled about being enrolled in Miss Claudine's than Emma or Charlie were. Until now, she'd sat in the backseat with her arms folded tightly and hadn't spoken more than a few tight-lipped hellos.

Lindsey looked at the tangle of traffic ahead of them and then turned to Emma and gave the thumbs-up sign. Emma smiled for the first time since she'd gotten into the car. The miracle that she had been praying for was happening—she was going to be spared the unspeakable horror of enrollment in yet another ballet school.

"We might as well just turn back now," Emma said seriously. "If you get a late start, well, you can forget about ever catching up, you're always behind the other students and it's . . . it's a nightmare."

Mrs. Clark turned around and eyed Emma skeptically. "I don't think being fifteen minutes late will make much difference," she commented flatly.

"You'd be surprised," said Emma. "Timing is everything in ballet."

"There's another thing, Mrs. Clark," Lindsey pressed, wanting to make the most of this possible opportunity. "We're ten years old already. That's way too late to start ballet lessons. All the great dancers start at four or five. A girl in our class has been taking lessons since she was three. She told me that in ballet terms we're practically ancient history . . . we're like baseball players who only learned to play when they were twenty or something. I mean, forget it, it's just too old, it's hopeless."

"They're right, Mom," Charlie insisted. "You know last year on *Search for Love* Reva Harris developed amnesia because she flubbed a big ballet audition, and she couldn't bear to live with the shame. Maybe she was late for her first class, or began classes when she was already ten, and her trouble started way back then."

"That's enough," said Mrs. Clark sternly, obviously rattled by the blare of car horns outside and the mutiny she sensed brewing inside the car. "People very rarely develop amnesia in real life, Charlie. It's mostly a TV disease. Did you ever personally know anyone who had amnesia?"

"I wish I had amnesia now so I could forget about ballet," Charlie said sourly.

"Ballet is a beautiful art form and great exercise," Mrs. Clark insisted as she edged the car slowly into the moving traffic in the next lane. "Even if you don't pursue it professionally, it develops poise, grace, and good posture. I wish I'd had ballet lessons when I was a girl."

16

"It's never too late, Mom. You can take the lessons, and we'll just look around the mall."

"Charlie." Her mother's exasperated tone told her to drop the subject.

Charlie turned to face the backseat. Emma was leaning over Lindsey at the side window as both girls strained to see what was blocking North Eastbridge Road. In the far lane a dented yellow Chevy was spewing gray-blue smoke from beneath its open hood. The driver, a tall, thin woman wearing a red knit cap and a matching red quilted jacket, paced back and forth. She wrung her hands as she stood helplessly watching the billowing cloud of fumes.

Lindsey nodded at Emma encouragingly. "That car's not going anywhere," she whispered, but when the two girls realized Charlie was looking at them, they stiffened and went back to looking out the window.

Charlie swiveled back around in her seat. She couldn't really blame Emma and Lindsey for being mad at her. After all, it was her mother who had contacted their parents and started this whole mess to begin with. Still, it wasn't really fair of them to be angry at her. Charlie was just as much a victim of her mother's zeal for ballet lessons as they were.

Charlie told herself she didn't like them, either, so it didn't matter, but the unfairness of being blamed for something that wasn't her fault gave her a bad feeling in her stomach. Despite herself, she wanted Emma and Lindsey to understand that if it were up to her, they'd all be home watching Saturday morning TV right now.

"Uh-oh," murmured Emma. Charlie looked out the window and saw a yellow tow truck making its way through the traffic. All too quickly it reached the trou-

17

bled car. A man jumped out, and in minutes he had the car hooked to the cables of his truck. The tall woman climbed into the truck beside him, talking to the man excitedly, and soon the truck was dragging the car out of the way.

"Thank goodness," sighed Mrs. Clark.

"Ohhhhh," moaned the three girls at once, sinking dejectedly into their seats. The cars began moving again, and it wasn't long before the gleaming, modern stores of the Eastbridge Mall came into view.

Emma stared out the window. She usually enjoyed going to the mall. Since she'd moved to Eastbridge from Manhattan last July, after her parents divorced, it was the only thing about Eastbridge she *did* enjoy.

There was a great shop where Emma could buy the dangly day-glo earrings she loved, and another one that sold oversized hand-painted, sparkly T-shirts and stretchy pants. Those were looks Emma felt good wearing—not like the boring crew-neck sweaters and jeans her new classmates at Eastbridge Elementary practically lived in.

Emma sighed to herself as they pulled into the circular entrance road that wrapped around the mall. She knew that this bout of ballet classes would end the same way as the last three times her mother enrolled her in classes. She'd find a zillion ways to avoid ballet class, including getting all the way up to the front door and then bolting. Finally the teacher would get the message that Emma had no intention of becoming a serious ballerina and would request—to Emma's great relief—that she be removed from class.

Emma wished her mother would get the message as well. But she never did. Mrs. Guthrie had taken years of lessons, and had wanted to be a dancer, but she'd had Emma instead. So now she was a literary agent, and Emma was supposed to be the dancer.

No matter how much Emma protested, her mother wouldn't listen. "You're thin and graceful like I was at your age," her mother would say. "You were born to dance." Emma didn't agree. Ballet just made her muscles ache and made her feel self-conscious and awkward. And she always seemed to be the one who was a step behind everyone else in the class. What made her happy was painting and sketching. She was going to be an artist, not a ballerina.

Mrs. Clark turned into the parking lot. Although it was only just after ten in the morning the lot was filling up quickly because it was Saturday.

"Here we are," Mrs. Clark said as she pulled into a parking space close to the rear entrance of the mall.

"We're here, all right," muttered Charlie, pulling herself out of the front seat.

Lindsey and Emma slid out of the backseat. Lindsey jammed her hands into the pockets of her blue stone-washed jean jacket and scowled. "I'm not wearing one of those tutu things," she growled to no one in particular.

"You wear leotards," Emma informed her. "They don't look too bad."

"Maybe on you they don't," sulked Lindsey, running a hand through her medium-length curly blond hair. "And they better not ask me to put my hair in a bun or something weird like that, because I won't." She scowled at her reflection in the car window. She couldn't picture her compact square body in a leotard, spinning gracefully across a stage.

20

"Look over there," Charlie said. Forgetting to give her the cold shoulder for the moment, Emma and Lindsey looked in the direction she was pointing and saw a tow truck with a dented yellow car attached to its cables. "That's the same car that was holding up traffic on the way over. I wonder what it's doing here."

Emma and Lindsey looked at her and shrugged. Then they remembered that they were angry and turned away, looking offended that Charlie had even spoken to them.

They weren't *really* angry at Charlie, but they felt they had to be mad at somebody and they'd get in trouble if they were rude to Mrs. Clark. So, without discussing it, they'd decided to make Charlie the object of their annoyance over this whole ballet disaster. Even though Emma and Lindsey had just about nothing in common, they were firmly united against their common enemy—Charlie.

"Come on, girls," Mrs. Clark encouraged. "This is going to be fun." The three girls just looked at her as if she was insane and followed sullenly as she led them through the door and into the brightly lit mall with its lanes of stores. Sprightly music wafted through the air around them. It seemed in sharp contrast to their own gloomy moods.

Lindsey lingered in front of John's Sporting Goods store and examined the goalie's helmet in the front window. If this ballet stuff interfered with her playing soccer, somebody was going to pay, she vowed.

Her father had gotten it into his head that Lindsey should be less of a tomboy and more ladylike the day she'd come home with a note from the principal, explaining that his daughter had been fighting with boys in the schoolyard.

The note made it sound so much worse than it had been. Lindsey had tried to explain that it had all started when they were playing soccer. She was goalie, and dumb Jonathan Smith kept insisting that his goal was good when she had clearly kicked it out. She let it go a couple of times, but by the third time enough was enough. They'd argued, she'd given him a little push, and he got all bent out of shape and pushed her back, and then Bob Myers had to get into the act and start shouting. That's when Mrs. Burr, the principal, walked over and blamed the whole stupid thing on Lindsey.

Ever since Lindsey's mother had died two years ago, her father had worried that she needed more feminine influences in her life. The note from Mrs. Burr just convinced him he was right. And then, on the very same day, Mrs. Clark had called up with the "perfect" solution—ballet lessons. Lindsey almost felt that it was a terrible plot designed to ruin her life, not to mention her chances of playing soccer after school.

"Come on," Mrs. Clark called. "It's nearly ten-thirty." Lindsey made fists in her pockets, bent her head, and caught up with the others.

They made their way down to the lower level of the mall. "Figures it would be down here with all the tacky stores," mumbled Emma as her eye followed the trail of signs: Ernie's Auto Parts; Howard Hardware; Paulsen's Hosiery; The Red Robin Coffee and Donut Shop.

It was easy to spot Miss Claudine's School of Ballet. Not only was the name lettered in large, swirling black script against a pink curtain in the storefront window, but a small sea of about twenty girls with their hair combed up and gathered into topknots stood in front of the door, holding their dance bags and waiting to get in.

Lindsey clutched the sleeve of Emma's jacket. "We've been saved! Miss Claudine died!"

"Don't say that," hushed Emma. "You can't wish someone dead. She was abducted by enemy agents."

"Okay, whatever," Lindsey agreed gleefully. "All that matters is she's not here."

Three

"Guess we'll have to go home," Charlie suggested to her mother as they stood in front of Miss Claudine's and looked at the group of girls waiting for the school to open.

"Let's stay a few minutes and see what happens," Mrs. Clark insisted.

"I'm sure she's not coming, Mom," Charlie argued. "The school's probably out of business already."

Charlie realized that her mother wasn't going to budge, so she wandered over to an appliance store and gazed longingly at the five superwide TV screens that were playing five different stations at once, all in color.

Just then a woman came hurrying toward the group at a fast clip. Her red coat was flying behind her. She pulled off her red hat as she broke into a run, sending her long ash-blond hair tumbling down to her waist.

"Pardonnez-moi, mesdemoiselles," the woman cried. *"Pardonnez-moi!"* The woman scurried to the front door of Miss Claudine's and whipped a ring of clattering keys from her large black pocketbook. *"Voilà!"* she exclaimed, unlocking the door and flinging it open dramatically.

"Hey, that's the woman with the broken-down car,"

Lindsey said to Emma. "She must have talked the tow-truck guy into driving her here."

"How could she talk him into anything?" Emma remarked. "She doesn't even speak English."

"Do you think that's Miss Claudine, herself?" asked Charlie, who had broken away from the bliss of the appliance store and rejoined Emma and Lindsey when the woman appeared. "She seems like some kind of a nut to me."

Emma and Lindsey nodded, forgetting again to snub Charlie. "She sure does," Lindsey agreed.

"She probably escaped from a French lunatic asylum," offered Emma dramatically.

"Mom, do you think it's safe to leave us here with her?" Charlie asked her mother. "What if one of us gets injured, and she can't call the hospital because she can't speak the language? It could be a tragedy. That happened on *The Spinning World* when Rex was hurt on the island of Hunjuju with people who only spoke Hunjujuan."

"Let's go," said Mrs. Clark, ignoring Charlie's plea. Charlie noticed that though her mother's voice was firm, she looked skeptical for the first time that day. Surely, Charlie reasoned hopefully, she had to realize that this Miss Claudine was a little on the eccentric side.

Mrs. Clark walked through the front door of Miss Claudine's School, and the girls, not seeing any way out, followed reluctantly behind.

Inside the studio, things were a whirl of activity. Girls ran in and out of a door that obviously led to the dressing room in search of pins, ribbons, and forgotten tights. Miss Claudine seemed oblivious to the chaos around her as she sat serenely behind a large, worn-looking desk, writing in an oversized notebook. Charlie surveyed the room. Behind Miss Claudine to the right was a door with frosted glass panels that had the word *office* written on it. Above Miss Claudine's head was the framed photo of a young woman wearing tap shoes, a leotard with a tuxedo jacket, and a plumed hat. There was an inscription on the photo that Charlie couldn't read. She assumed it was one of Miss Claudine's friends or former students.

"Excuse me," Mrs. Clark said, stepping forward.

Miss Claudine looked up from her book. She seemed startled at first but quickly focused on the newcomers. *"Bonjour, mesdemoiselles, madame,"* she greeted them as she rose majestically from behind the desk with her arms outstretched in a welcoming gesture. The three girls instinctively took a step backward, half afraid she was going to gather them together in an embrace.

None of them had ever seen anyone like Miss Claudine. She seemed neither young nor old. They certainly couldn't picture her being anyone's mother. She had pale skin, and her nose and chin were somewhat pointy. She wasn't exactly pretty, but her blue eyes seemed to shine, and her long ash-blond hair swirled around her shoulders when she spoke. She was tall and thin and wore a lavender leotard over which she'd wrapped a calf-length dance skirt of the same color. "Have you come to register for classes?" she asked.

"Thank goodness," whispered Charlie under her breath, relieved that Miss Claudine spoke at least a few words of English.

Mrs. Clark told Miss Claudine that they had come to register and gave their names and addresses. Miss Claudine took it all down in her big notebook and then surveyed the three girls. She walked around them three times with her arms folded, looking them over.

"Mesdemoiselles Emma, Lindsey, and Charlotte," she mused in her melodic voice, as if entering each of their names in her memory.

"I hate the name Charlotte," protested Charlie, wincing at the sound of the name she'd been given in honor of her great-grandmother. Her mother frowned at her, and she added more politely, "Please call me Charlie."

"Non, non, ma chérie," said Miss Claudine. "Charlotte is a beautiful name. It's French. A beautiful name from the richest language on earth."

"My name is Charlie," Charlie insisted through clenched teeth.

"I cannot have such a name for one of my ballerinas," Miss Claudine objected pleasantly. "I will have to call you Mademoiselle Clark until you come to appreciate the elegance of your true name. Perhaps studying ballet will open your eyes to the Charlotte hiding within you."

Charlie looked to her mother for aid, but Mrs. Clark simply winked at her daughter with eyes full of laughter. It was clear to Charlie that her mother was not sympathetic. Miss Claudine had obviously won her over already.

"Miss Claudine," called a slim, pretty girl of about eleven or twelve with dark hair drawn up sleekly in a bun. "I think we're ready." The girl's gaze fell on Charlie, Emma, and Lindsey. She tilted back her head and narrowed her eyes as she looked at them. Her expression made them feel as if they were mangy dogs who had somehow wandered into the studio. They glared back at her with equal dislike.

27

"*Merci*, Danielle," Miss Claudine answered the girl. "We will begin momentarily."

Miss Claudine reached into a closet by the front door and brought out three plastic-wrapped packages containing powder blue leotards with matching tights, and three pairs of soft pink slippers.

"These are included in your fee," Miss Claudine assured Mrs. Clark who had finished filling in information cards for the girls and now looked ready to leave. "Class lasts until twelve-forty-five. That gives us an hour for ballet and forty-five minutes for my specialty—ballet culture."

Ballet culture? thought Charlie with alarm. But she never even got a chance to ask what it was.

"I'll pick you up at one," Mrs. Clark told the girls as she headed for the door. "Have fun."

"Thanks, Mom," said Charlie flatly. "Thanks loads." Annoyed as Charlie was with her mother, she didn't want to see her leave. It was as if her mother was her last link with civilization. Now she was alone in this strange studio with two hostile classmates and . . . Miss Claudine.

Lindsey opened her package and held the leotard out in front of her by two fingers, as if it was a wet rat. "This is baby blue," she said, disgusted by the dainty color. "I thought we would at least wear black."

Miss Claudine ignored her comment. Instead she grabbed Lindsey's outstretched arm. "*C'est bon,*" she gasped. "Very good! You have a natural reach." Lindsey looked around for a way to escape Miss Claudine's grasp, but the teacher didn't let go.

"*Attention,* class," Miss Claudine called, gathering the class around her. "I want you to look at our new student, Mademoiselle Lindsey. This is the type of full reach I've been encouraging you to develop. I can tell just from looking at her that Mademoiselle Lindsey will quickly develop a lovely port de bras."

Lindsey's eyes went wide in horror, and she felt the heat of a blush rushing to her face. How could Miss Claudine make such a mortifying comment about her bra size—and in front of all these strangers! She didn't even wear a bra! This woman really *was* some kind of kook. She yanked her arm away from Miss Claudine and crossed her arms over her chest.

Emma looked at Lindsey's stunned expression and then at Charlie's horrified one. "She means you hold your arms gracefully," she whispered quickly to Lindsey. "It's ballet talk."

Miss Claudine clapped her hands, and her students scampered into the large, mirrored studio behind them. "Danielle, show the *mesdemoiselles* to the dressing room where they will put on their leotards and slippers," she said.

"Follow me," Danielle ordered haughtily, leading them to the room they'd seen the other ballet students dashing in and out of earlier.

Inside the small dressing room the girls changed into their leotards. Charlie felt weird taking off her clothes in front of strangers, especially strangers who weren't being exactly friendly to her. She put the tights on first and then pulled the leotard up under her shirt before taking it off. Standing on tiptoes, she checked herself in the small mirror. She decided it could have been worse; she didn't look that bad.

Emma changed quickly, paying no attention to anyone, and then leaned against the wall with her arms

folded in disgust and waited for the others. After a few seconds of waiting, she reached into her pocketbook and pulled out a tube of thick black mascara and began applying it.

Lindsey changed slowly, facing the wall. When she had her leotard and tights on, she glanced quickly in the mirror. Her broad, square shoulders and straight hips looked all wrong to her in this feminine outfit. Plus, the port de bras incident had made her doubly self-conscious. She was sure everyone would take one look at her and start laughing.

Lindsey was desperate. How could she go out there looking and feeling so dumb? Then she spotted the long red Yankees T-shirt she'd been wearing and quickly slipped it on over the leotard. It fell just past her hips. She looked in the mirror again and decided that with her T-shirt on she could live with the leotard and tights.

"You can't wear that," said Danielle, pointing at Lindsey's T-shirt. "Miss Claudine has to be able to see if your placement is correct."

"My placement is just fine, thanks," snapped Lindsey, not having the faintest idea of what Danielle was talking about.

Danielle placed her hands on her hips and stood in front of the doorway. "You're not wearing that T-shirt. Take it off."

"No way," growled Lindsey, facing Danielle nose to nose.

"Miss Claudine!" yelled Danielle. "Oh, Miss Claudine!"

Miss Claudine appeared in the doorway behind Danielle. "*Mesdemoiselles,* what is the problem?" she asked with genuine concern.

"She insists on wearing this ridiculous baseball T-shirt over her leotard, Miss Claudine," Danielle said shrilly. "I told her it was out of the question."

"Who died and put you in charge of the world?" Emma snapped at the girl. Danielle narrowed her eyes and smirked back at Emma.

"I don't see what difference it makes," Charlie spoke up, not wanting to look like a wimp just standing there speechless.

"Of course, you don't," Danielle said in a superior tone. "You clearly don't know the first thing about the dance." Charlie certainly couldn't argue with that.

"*Merci,* Danielle, I will settle this," said Miss Claudine. "Now be a dear and go get the class warmed up. I will be there in a minute."

"I'd be glad to, Miss Claudine." Danielle threw the girls an I-told-you-so look and swirled out of the room.

Miss Claudine put her graceful hand on Lindsey's shoulder. "You must understand, *chérie,* that I have to be able to see if you are positioning your body correctly. Otherwise, you might injure yourself. It is hard for me to see if you are executing the moves correctly when you are hidden under that big shirt."

Lindsey folded her arms tightly. "I'm not going out there dressed in this twerpy outfit," she said sulkily. "I'm just not. That's all."

Miss Claudine stepped back and studied Lindsey. "Such a strong, sturdy body—you should be proud to show it off."

Lindsey just stood with her arms folded, looking at the floor. Part of her wanted to be agreeable, but a bigger part felt too embarrassed to be seen without her T-shirt.

Miss Claudine shook her head with a resigned air. "Very well, one step at a time," she said with a deep sigh. "Wear the shirt. If that is what it takes to get you started in your love for the ballet, then it doesn't pay for me to be rigid. Ballet dancers are like flowers. Each has her own gift, but each must unfold, petal by petal, and bloom in her own time."

With a sweep of her arm, Miss Claudine beckoned them to follow. "Come, the dance awaits," she said simply, and then turned and walked toward the ballet studio, not bothering to notice whether or not they were with her.

Charlie was the first to follow along behind Miss Claudine. She took her place at the barre, facing the wall. Danielle was leading the class through a series of what looked to Charlie like contorted deep knee bends. The girl beside her seemed to rise and descend effortlessly. Charlie concentrated on Danielle and tried to follow her every move. It seemed that Miss Claudine expected them to pick up the steps on their own, by watching.

"Backs straight, heads high," Miss Claudine encouraged them, relieving Danielle of her position. "When you plié, pretend there is an invisible string attached to your head, and it is pulling you to the ceiling."

Lindsey had taken a spot several girls away from Charlie, next to the door. She attempted the graceful movement but she did it too rapidly, as if she were in gym class. She definitely didn't have the flowing grace of the other students in the class. This was turning out to be just as big a drag as she'd expected.

Looking for a sympathetic face, Lindsey looked over her shoulder for Emma. She'd thought Emma was right

33

behind her, but now she didn't see her anywhere. Strange, she thought.

Suddenly Lindsey heard a *pssst* sound. She turned to the doorway. At first she didn't see anyone, but in the next minute she saw Emma peek around the corner. Lindsey realized that Emma had changed back into her clothes.

She shot Emma a questioning glance, but Emma ducked back behind the door. Lindsey looked to Miss Claudine, but the ballet teacher was now bending and rising along with the class.

Lindsey looked back at the doorway. Emma's head darted out and then back. Then all Lindsey saw was Emma's small hand as she stuck it into the doorway and waved good-bye.

Lindsey couldn't believe it. Emma was making a break for it!

Four

Lindsey looked quickly around the studio. Miss Claudine was busy repositioning the feet of a girl at the far end of the room.

She glanced back at the empty doorway where Emma had been standing a second ago. If Emma wasn't staying in class, why should she? She thought of signaling Charlie, but then decided against it. She wasn't sure enough of Charlie. Besides, the two of them wouldn't be able to get out unnoticed.

With another quick check over her shoulder, Lindsey slipped out of the studio to the front room. She caught sight of Emma's purple jacket through the glass of the front door as it swung shut behind her.

Lindsey didn't know what to do. She wanted to change into her regular clothes, but there was no time. If she didn't leave now, she'd lose track of Emma, and, somehow, wandering around the mall by herself didn't seem like much fun to Lindsey.

There was no time for indecision. Miss Claudine might realize she was gone any minute and come looking for her. It was now or never.

Lindsey heard the sound of someone putting on a scratchy-sounding classical record, and then Miss Claudine began to speak. "Danielle will now perform the role of the dying swan princess from *Swan Lake* for us," she began. "I have re-choreographed the ballet so that none of it is danced *en pointe*. Young ankles can't take the strain of toe dancing. At this year's recital, many of you will play the parts of her swan attendants."

That was all it took to send Lindsey sprinting out the front door. No way was she dancing around like a duck, attending to Danielle. "Emma, wait up," she called to the girl who was walking quickly away from Miss Claudine's.

Emma whirled around and looked at Lindsey with a panicked expression. Instead of stopping, she started walking even faster.

"Hold up," called Lindsey, running after her.

Emma broke into a run, but Lindsey caught up to her easily. "I'm not going back. Don't try to make me," Emma snapped when Lindsey was alongside her.

"Are you crazy? I don't want you to go back. I'm busting out with you," Lindsey explained.

Emma stopped and caught her breath as she studied Lindsey suspiciously. "Aren't you afraid of getting in trouble?"

"I don't know. Aren't you?"

Emma shrugged. "I'm always in trouble. It sort of doesn't bother me anymore. It seems to me that you have two choices: either be in trouble all the time, or always do what other people want you to do. I'd rather be in trouble."

Lindsey had to think about that one. In all honesty, she hated being in trouble. The thought of it usually made her sick to her stomach. She'd never met anyone who didn't care. Most kids she knew did everything in their power to avoid getting into trouble.

Lindsey wondered if Emma was what her father would call "a bad influence," because right now Lindsey didn't care about getting into trouble. Something about Emma made her feel that it wasn't anything to worry about.

"I guess I'd rather get into trouble than take that stupid ballet class," she admitted.

Emma smiled, and Lindsey noticed that she looked very different when she wasn't wearing her sour, serious expression—pretty, even. "Do you *believe* that Danielle character? What a jerk!" Emma said.

" 'Yes, Miss Claudine. No, Miss Claudine,' " Lindsey mimicked Danielle in a high squeal. Emma laughed and Lindsey laughed along with her. It suddenly seemed to them as if Miss Claudine's was a terrible experience that was now safely behind them—something it was now okay to joke about.

They strolled through the mall with the delicious feeling of being on a great adventure. It was as if the mall was some strange, new land just full of fascinating things to explore. They had the feeling that anything could happen.

Emma stopped and breathed deeply. "A mall is really a wonderful place," she said happily. "You could almost live here. Think of it. There are all kinds of food stands with all the best foods—hot dogs, french fries, pizza, ice cream. And the big stores, like Horner's, have everything else you need. You can watch TV in the electronics departments, the best, biggest TVs around. You can try on expensive stuff, like dresses that you can't afford to buy. There are puppies and kittens in the pet department. It's almost like having a private zoo. And there's always stuff going on like fashion shows, rock bands, and contests."

The idea of living in the mall suddenly struck Emma as the most wonderful fantasy in the world. No rules, no school, and—as long as she was careful to avoid a certain part of the mall—no ballet class. "You could probably even sleep in those big, fancy beds in the furniture department at night."

Lindsey wasn't so sure. "I think they have night watchmen, but maybe if you hid under the bed when they made their rounds, it might be possible. You wouldn't get much sleep, though, if you had to keep jumping under the bed, and if you did fall asleep, then you'd get caught."

"Oh, I'd be able to figure something out," said Emma, not wanting a troublesome detail like night watchmen to spoil her fantasy. She could actually picture herself lounging in one of those big canopy beds in Horner's furniture department. Or maybe she'd rather have the one she'd seen with the zebra-skin headboard. That was the beauty of living in a mall—you could try out a different bed every night.

"Malls are the one thing I love about Eastbridge," she told Lindsey. "There were no really good malls back in Manhattan. You had to travel all over the place to find the different things you wanted."

"How come you moved?" asked Lindsey.

"Parents divorced," Emma answered matter-of-factly. "Dad stayed in the city, so I still go in to see him a lot. I'm moving back to the city as soon as I'm eighteen. That's where I really belong."

Lindsey decided that Emma was right; she did seem more like a city kid. She certainly wasn't like anyone

Lindsey knew at Eastbridge Elementary. She seemed older, somehow. The makeup and styles she wore even made her *look* older.

"I think I belong right here," Lindsey said, "or maybe on a horse ranch. When my mother was alive we went to a horse ranch in Texas for a week once, and I could definitely see myself living there. All we did all day was take care of the horses and ride them around on the trails. I rode this little pony named Scamp. It was great. I've only been to Manhattan once, but it seems pretty crowded and dirty to me."

"To each his own," Emma said lightly, not offended. She took pride in the fact that not everyone liked the city. Her father said it took a special kind of person to appreciate its pace. "You *are* more the outdoors type," she added, "though you sure don't look it in that getup."

Lindsey looked at herself in the store window, suddenly remembering that she was wearing a T-shirt, tights, and ballet slippers. "Do I look too weird? I mean, they won't arrest me or anything, will they?"

"Nah, nobody's even paying attention," Emma said. "The T-shirt makes the outfit look kind of cool."

"I feel like a giant pixie," Lindsey complained.

That made Emma laugh. "Don't worry, the T-shirt really saves it," she assured her.

Lindsey wasn't the kind of girl Emma usually liked. In fact, she had always detested jocks. It seemed to Emma that most jocks tried to make you feel like a wimp just because you weren't interested in sports. But somehow Lindsey was different. She just was what she was and didn't seem to be judging Emma for being different. And if there was one thing Emma hated more than anything else in the world, it was being judged.

It occurred to Emma that she was very glad Lindsey had followed her out of Miss Claudine's. It would have been kind of depressing to roam around the mall all by herself. She'd probably have spent the whole time thinking about how much she hated ballet and about how all her other ballet classes had been such disasters—teachers and students judging everything about you every second, the way you stood, the way you moved, even the way you held your hands. It was just a festival of being picked apart by strangers. Who needed it?

Emma was seized by the urge to do something nice for Lindsey. She looked at Lindsey's pale, lightly freckled face beneath the tousle of blond curls. "You know what you need?" she said finally.

"What?"

"Makeup."

"Oh, gee, thanks a lot," Lindsey said sarcastically. "Maybe I should just wear a mask. Would that make you happy?"

"Don't get insulted. I didn't mean it that way," Emma explained. "Just about everyone looks better with makeup. I know that I do."

Lindsey looked at the thick clumps of mascara on Emma's lashes. Emma's greenish eyes did look brighter than they had before she framed them with the mascara. "Maybe it looks okay on you, but it would just look weird on me. Besides, my father would kill me if he saw me with makeup."

"My mother doesn't let me wear makeup, either. That's why I carry it with me in my pocketbook."

"What about when you get home?"

"I just wash it off before I go home. Simple."

"I wouldn't even know how to put it on, anyway."

"That's what I'm here for," said Emma grandly, "to show you. Being in a mall is like being in makeup heaven. Samples of every makeup you can possibly think of are here. There's a great Sparkle Glow counter upstairs at Nevins Department Store. I go there all the time."

Normally Lindsey would have thought it a lot more fun to browse through the sports departments of the big stores, but she knew Emma would never be interested. Besides, it seemed like part of this strange adventure to do something different.

"What the heck," she said. "We have almost two hours to kill until Mrs. Clark picks us up, anyway. . . . Hey, what are we going to do about that?"

Emma shrugged. "I guess we can go back there and stand out front and act like we'd been inside the whole time."

"Do you think Charlie will tell on us?" Lindsey wondered aloud, letting a twinge of her old fear of getting into trouble creep back in.

"You mean 'Mademoiselle Charlotte'?" giggled Emma. "I don't know. She might. I can't really tell."

"I can't tell, either," Lindsey agreed. "I don't know Charlie too well even though she's been in my class for the last two years. I feel kind of bad. We were pretty mean to her."

"Are you kidding?" Emma protested indignantly. "This whole mess is all her fault."

"Come on, Emma, you can't honestly say that. I mean, what was she supposed to do if her mother forced her to take ballet lessons? It's not like she begged to be enrolled at Miss Claudine's and insisted we come with her."

"Then whose fault is it?" Emma asked.

"I guess it's her mother's fault," Lindsey answered. "And our parents' fault. They could have said no when she called up. She didn't put a gun to their heads or anything."

"That's what really bugs me about parents," Emma confessed. "They're always acting like they know what's best for you. When I said I didn't want to take ballet lessons, my mother should have just said okay, fine."

"I know, but sometimes they do know more than you do," Lindsey said.

Emma looked at her as if she were insane. "If my parents know so much, then how come they got divorced?" she challenged. "That was a pretty dumb move, if you ask me."

Not waiting for Lindsey to respond, Emma ran over to a poster store and began looking at the pictures in the window. Lindsey followed, and they stood for a while, staring at the posters without talking.

Lindsey had an idea of how Emma felt. She remembered how she'd felt two years ago when her mother had died of cancer. Besides the sadness, it was the first time it had occurred to her that her father didn't have the answer to every single one of life's problems. She knew now that it had been babyish to expect him to be able to solve a problem that the doctors couldn't solve. Still, at the time, it had frightened her that her father was powerless to stop her mother from dying. It was scary to think of your parents as people who didn't have all the answers.

"Stuff happens," Lindsey said, "stuff even parents don't know what to do about."

"That's what I'm saying," Emma insisted. "If they don't know everything, they shouldn't go around acting like they do."

Lindsey didn't know how to argue the point, but she wasn't comfortable with the idea. Despite the fact that they weren't perfect, she liked the feeling that her father and teachers knew a little more than she did. It gave her a safe feeling to think that the adults around her had a pretty good idea of what life was about. And in her heart she believed that, in general, they did.

Emma and Lindsey left the poster store and continued walking until they stood in front of the entrance of Nevins. "The Sparkle Glow counter is on the second floor. Come on, you'll love it," said Emma eagerly.

Lindsey was once again filled with a great sense of freedom. "Boy, am I glad we decided to ditch that class," she said. "This is fun."

"Yeah," Emma agreed. "I wonder what poor old Charlie is doing now."

Five

Charlie watched as Danielle fluttered to the floor and died. The class applauded politely. *"C'est bon,* Danielle," Miss Claudine praised, "very good. You were a bit unsure of yourself in some parts, but you've just learned the dance. With more practice you will be a very beautiful swan princess indeed."

Danielle rose to her feet and smiled at Miss Claudine. Charlie had to admit she was impressed. Danielle was a graceful dancer even if she did always wear an unbearable look of superiority on her face.

"Arabesques now, *mesdemoiselles,"* said Miss Claudine. She stood in front of the class and extended one leg gracefully into the air behind her. With one flowing movement, her left arm floated up in front of her and her right, behind. The expression on her face was that of calm concentration. She looked to Charlie like a lovely statue.

The girls in the class followed Miss Claudine's example, except that they steadied themselves at the barre with one hand. Though extended legs jutted out at odd angles, Charlie noticed they all managed to stay balanced.

Charlie leaned forward and tried the arabesque. Her standing leg shook uncontrollably as she tried to raise

the other one off the ground. Every time her back foot rose more than two inches, she would start to lose her balance and have to put it down. No one, not even Miss Claudine, seemed to notice.

This was the story of her life, Charlie thought as she wobbled uncontrollably on her one foot; she was the klutziest kid she knew. Her brothers played every sport going, and they were good at all of them. Her parents played tennis every Saturday, and they were always the ones who got up a volleyball game in the summer, or a neighborhood touch-football match in the fall.

Even though she resembled her father, it had occurred to Charlie that maybe she'd been adopted. How else could she explain the fact that she was so completely different from the rest of her family? She couldn't dribble a basketball, hit a baseball, or kick a soccer ball. And it wasn't that she hadn't tried. Her mother had forced her to try out for every after-school team and league she could find. Mrs. Clark's attempts to separate Charlie from her beloved TV set hadn't begun with ballet. Ballet was just the latest in an endless series of group activities Mrs. Clark wanted Charlie to become involved in.

Luckily for Charlie, she never got past the tryout stage in sports. Once the humiliation of striking out, or having to chase a rolling basketball across the court, or whatever, was over, Charlie would be told politely that she hadn't made the team and she could return to the fun of watching TV. But now, with ballet, there were no tryouts, no team to be rejected from. She would just have to be terrible at it and continue to be terrible forever. The thought made Charlie's leg shake even harder.

Miss Claudine had been holding her arabesque. Now she flowed effortlessly out of the position and the class followed. "Thank goodness that's over," thought Charlie. She looked over her shoulder to see how Lindsey and Emma were doing.

It was then that she realized they were gone!

A cold chill of panic ran up Charlie's spine. She'd assumed they were right there in the studio with her all this time. She looked around the room again to be sure. No, they were definitely not there.

Charlie's mind raced wildly. How did they get out? Where could they have gone? What would her mother say when she came to pick them up?

"And again, arabesques," said Miss Claudine, "but this time we will concentrate on balance. I want you all to step away from the barre, toward the center of the room."

The girls spaced themselves out evenly throughout the room and followed Miss Claudine in doing a free-standing arabesque. Not knowing what else to do, Charlie tried the arabesque again, but this time more than just her leg was shaking. She was shaking all over. She lifted her back leg and quickly put it down. She tried again, and this time she stuck her arms out to her sides and flapped them around in a determined attempt to balance herself.

"Shoulders down, heads up high," Miss Claudine coached as she surveyed her class from her arabesque position. "You are all swans, beautiful, graceful swans."

Charlie couldn't think of herself as a swan. She had too much else on her mind—like what she was going to do about the missing Lindsey and Emma. Her mother would kill her. Even though it wasn't her fault,

Charlie was just certain that her mother would blame her for letting them escape. She had to somehow get them back to Miss Claudine's before her mother returned to the mall to pick them up.

But how? It was hard to come up with a plan while trying to lift one foot in the air. Feebly, she managed to stand with her back leg bent and slightly lifted behind her. She knew she didn't look too graceful, but she couldn't worry about it now. She had to find a way to sneak out of class so she could go in search of Emma and Lindsey.

She knew Lindsey had been standing closest to the door, and Emma had probably never even entered the studio. That's how they'd gotten away so quietly. But Charlie was in the middle of the class. She couldn't just up and walk out.

Charlie looked at Miss Claudine who was now intently working out a series of steps by herself in the corner of the room as the girls continued to practice their arabesques. She didn't even realize that Emma and Lindsey were gone. It was as if the minute she stepped into the studio she became completely focused on ballet and nothing else. Besides, she wasn't used to seeing Emma and Lindsey—or Charlie, for that matter—so their absence probably didn't really register with her.

But could Charlie get away with just walking out? Even if she could have, she didn't have the nerve to try. No, she would have to figure some other way to get out unnoticed.

She tried to think. What did people do on TV? They created a disturbance. Reva Harris had once started screaming that she saw a ghost when she wanted her boyfriend to be able to sneak away from the supposedly haunted house. While everyone was looking at her, Lance sneaked out the back door.

Somehow Charlie didn't think that would translate too well to her situation. If she started screaming, everyone would be staring at her and she'd hardly be able to sneak away then. Plus, Miss Claudine would tell her mother, and she'd wind up in even worse trouble.

Maybe the trick was to get someone *else* to create a disturbance while you ran away. Since she had no one to help her, the situation felt just about hopeless to Charlie—but suddenly inspiration struck, or rather it popped its head out.

She noticed a small, gray mouse sticking its head out of a loose piece of plasterboard in the corner of the studio by the door. Charlie watched as it cautiously began to make its way along the baseboard toward the pink trash can at the other end of the studio. A torn cellophane wrapper still containing bits of an old coffee cake lay next to the can. It was obviously the prize the mouse was after.

The girls were now spread out around the room, stretching. No one seemed to notice the mouse as it stopped every few feet, sniffed, then scurried forward toward the wrapper.

Knowing a good opportunity when she saw it, Charlie tapped the girl next to her. The girl shot her an annoyed glance, but when Charlie pointed in the direction of the mouse, her eyes went wide with horror.

"Ewwww," she squealed, jumping back and pointing at the mouse. The girls near her stopped what they were doing and looked at the mouse. Two of them ran to the other side of the room. The rest of the class quickly followed as one by one they became aware of the small

furry creature. They stood huddled together, hopping up and down unhappily.

"*Mesdemoiselles,* what is the meaning of this outburst?" asked Miss Claudine. "What is going on?"

"A mouse, Miss Claudine," the girls shouted.

"What babies!" said Danielle before Miss Claudine could react. "It's more afraid of you than you are of it. I can just chase it right back into its hole."

Danielle ran up to the mouse which had frozen in its tracks along the baseboard. It did seem frightened but it didn't run back into its hole. Panicked, it scurried out into the middle of the ballet studio.

"*Aaaahhhh!*" The girls screamed and ran in all directions. The mouse, terrified and confused, ran in circles under their feet.

"*Mesdemoiselles,* please control yourselves," yelled Miss Claudine, clapping her hands for order. "It's just a little mouse."

It was no use. The girls were in a complete panic, screaming and running around the studio. Charlie knew this was her perfect chance. Though she wasn't really afraid of the mouse, she covered her mouth with her hand and began screaming, "A mouse! A mouse!" blending in with the general commotion.

She ran closer and closer to the door. Then, with one burst of courage, she ran through the doorway into the front room and then straight out the glass front door into the mall.

Charlie kept running until she was almost ten stores away from Miss Claudine's. Finally she had to stop to catch her breath. Clutching her sides, she looked behind her. The mall was now full of shoppers, but no one seemed to be paying any attention to her. No one, that

was, except two little boys who stood and stared at her with bewildered eyes. Charlie realized they were staring at her because she was dressed in a leotard, tights and ballet slippers.

The reality of what she'd done hit Charlie. She'd escaped from Miss Claudine's, but now she was stuck walking around the mall in a ballet outfit. And how on earth was she ever going to find Emma and Lindsey in a mall this size?

Six

Charlie plopped down wearily on one of the cedar benches that lined the small decorative pool at the center of the mall. To the left of her sat an elderly couple who were resting from their morning of shopping. To her right was a woman who had a baby in a stroller and was wiping the sticky faces of her little girl and boy.

This is ridiculous, thought Charlie, sitting with her chin propped in her hands. *I'll never find them. I never realized that the Eastbridge Mall was so humongous.*

She'd been searching for Emma and Lindsey for almost a half hour with no luck. It seemed to Charlie, she'd been looking for them for days. Every moment had been torture as she tried to ignore the stares of shoppers who wondered why she was walking around the mall in a leotard and ballet slippers.

At first Charlie had concocted a story in her head in which she was a Russian ballet star who was escaping to the United States. She pursed her lips and scowled, hoping her expression conveyed the fact that she had important things on her mind. But one look in a store mirror convinced her that she didn't look a thing like a prima ballerina—not with her red hair held off her face with bobbie pins and the slippers that flapped on her feet ever so slightly when she walked.

Then she decided to imagine she was Reva Harris. Reva would have looked so breathtaking in a leotard, and would have carried herself with such self-assurance, that people would have no choice but to stare at her out of sheer admiration. Charlie tossed her head back saucily and took a deep breath. For a moment the petite ten-year-old disappeared, and a stunning brunette took her place—in Charlie's imagination at least. She tried to accept the curiosity of the shoppers as proof of their inability to hide their awe at her beauty.

That lasted for about five minutes. Charlie just couldn't convince herself it was true. Every store window reflected the truth back at her. Although she looked perfectly fine as a ten-year-old, she was no Reva Harris.

Charlie slumped down on the bench and wiggled her toes. Her feet were starting to hurt. Ballet slippers obviously weren't built for walking through every single inch of the Eastbridge Mall.

She closed her eyes for a moment, and when she opened them—there they were! She saw Emma and Lindsey walking out of Nevins Department Store all the way at the other end of the corridor. They were a good ten stores away, but there was no mistaking Emma's purple jacket and Lindsey's baby-blue legs.

Charlie jumped up and raced toward them, her ballet slippers slapping the hard cement floor. She couldn't let them get away now that she'd found them. As she got closer she could see they were laughing and having a great time.

They stopped to buy a hot dog at a stand outside of Nevins. Good, she'd be able to catch up to them.

Suddenly Charlie came to a screeching halt. Just

three stores away from Nevins was a video arcade and out of it walked a group of five boys from her class at Eastbridge Elementary. In the front of the group was Mark Johnson, the only boy Charlie didn't think was a total jerk. In fact, she liked Mark and thought he was cute. He reminded her a little of Lance Pembrook, Reva's boyfriend, with his curly black hair and dimpled chin.

The boys were being their usual selves—punching one another and jumping around or slumping along, their hands shoved in their pockets. Only Mark moved in a way that Charlie thought resembled human behavior.

The problem was—the boys were heading straight for Charlie! She felt her heart race as she was seized with complete panic. It didn't matter if she *should* care whether or not the boys saw her in her leotard, she did care and she had to get out of there—and fast!

Charlie looked around quickly. To her left was a pizza parlor. It was risky to duck in there. It was completely open, with only striped pillars separating it from the mall. Besides, the boys might be headed straight for it.

To her right was a small clothing store called Barb's Boutique. There wasn't much chance of the boys going in there. Ahead of her she saw Emma and Lindsey sitting on a bench, eating their hot dogs. With any luck the boys would pass right by the boutique, and she could still catch up to Emma and Lindsey.

She had to move quickly before the boys saw her. Charlie bolted across the corridor and through the glass door into Barb's Boutique. She hovered at the side of the door, peering out of the corner to see what the boys did.

Good, she thought, *they're walking straight on by.* But then they stopped right in front of the boutique. Charlie flattened herself against the side of the door so they wouldn't see her. One of the boys pointed to the pizzeria. After a brief discussion, which seemed, to Charlie, to take forever, they turned and went in for some pizza.

Darn, Charlie thought angrily. Now she'd have to wait in the boutique until they were done. If she went out, they'd definitely spot her.

"Look at that girl," a voice behind her said. Charlie whirled around and saw a woman with silver hair swept high on top of her head standing with a short saleswoman with bright orange hair and black-rimmed glasses. They were both staring intently at Charlie. She felt like a trapped animal. There was no place to hide and no place to run.

"That girl is just about the same size as my granddaughter," the silver-haired woman said, pointing at Charlie. "How old are you, dear?" she asked.

"Ten, last June," Charlie answered, trying to sound casual and calm.

"I knew it," said the woman happily. "Janine is also ten." She walked closer to Charlie and looked her over seriously. "Are ten-year-olds wearing ballet outfits these days?" she asked without a trace of sarcasm. "It's so difficult to keep up with trends when you're my age. Perhaps I should buy Janine ballet wear as a gift."

"Oh, no, no," Charlie said. "She'd hate that." The woman eyed her, confused. "You see, I take ballet class," Charlie explained. "I'm just . . . um . . . um . . . I'm on a break."

56

Charlie checked over her shoulder. The boys were still sitting at the front table of the pizza parlor.

"Would you mind trying on a few things?" the woman asked. "I'm visiting my daughter and Janine in Chicago this weekend, and I just can't decide what to bring her."

Trying on clothes was the last thing Charlie wanted to do, but if she didn't, the saleslady certainly wouldn't let her hang around the store for much longer. "Sure," she said, forcing herself to smile. "I'd be glad to."

"Just these few things," said the woman, turning and gathering an armload of dresses she'd laid out on the counter.

The saleslady took the dresses from her and loaded them into Charlie's arms. "The dressing room is to your left, hon," she said, directing Charlie to a tiny cubicle with a blue curtain in front of it.

Charlie staggered under the weight of the dresses. She could barely fit them all into the cramped dressing room. She pulled the first dress on over her leotard. It had puffed sleeves and a yellow pouf skirt with a crinoline that scratched at the waist.

"Raise your arms a bit, dear," the woman said as Charlie walked out of the dressing room. Feeling ridiculous, Charlie raised her arms over her head. "No, somehow it's just not Janine," the woman commented.

Charlie tried on five more dresses. None of them met with the woman's approval. Charlie was getting tired—and bored. She wanted to get out of there.

The sixth outfit Charlie tried on was a long orange-and-black tiger-striped top with matching stretch pants. A sequined tiger was machine embroidered on the front, with fake green stones for the eyes. The pants and

sleeves both hung long on Charlie's petite frame. Charlie hoped, for Janine's sake, that the silver-haired woman would hate this horrible outfit as much as she did.

"This is very with it," the saleslady commented when Charlie appeared in the pantsuit. "Animal prints are absolutely all the rage. We'll be glad to alter the sleeves and pants for you."

Charlie wanted to check and see if the boys were still eating pizza, so she pretended to be modeling the outfit and walked over by the door. A quick peek told her they were gone. She had to get out of there. "I have to go now," she said, "my break is over."

"Oh, couldn't you stay for just a few more outfits?" the woman requested.

Just then the little bell above the door tinkled. A customer was coming into the shop. Charlie looked over to the door and went pale. It was Mrs. Green, her mother's best friend!

Mrs. Green went right to the front counter and began looking over the jewelry in the case. She hadn't seen Charlie, but it wouldn't be long before she did. Charlie couldn't let that happen.

"I'll try on a few more," Charlie whispered to the woman while the saleslady went off to attend to Mrs. Green. "There are some nice outfits on that rack over there," she continued to whisper, pointing to a rack of girls' clothing behind the woman. "Why don't you pick out a few more?"

"Good idea," the woman whispered back, "but why are we whispering?"

"I'm just a little hoarse all of a sudden," Charlie lied, rubbing her throat.

The woman nodded and turned to look through the rack of dresses. Charlie immediately crouched low behind a round rack of suede jackets and crept toward the door. In a second she pulled the door open and ran out into the mall.

"Stop that kid!" she heard the saleslady yell as she raced down the first corridor and slid on her slick shoes around the corner. At that moment she realized that, technically speaking, she had just stolen the ugly tiger pantsuit. Charlie had never stolen a thing in her life, and if she'd ever been tempted to, this outfit was the last thing on earth she'd steal.

Charlie ran and ran, without looking back, until her lungs were ready to burst. Ducking behind a directory sign, she finally stopped and checked behind her. No one was after her. She'd escaped.

Charlie held her aching sides as she caught her breath. How had all of this gotten so out of hand? This morning she'd been your regular all-American couch potato. Now, here she was an escapee from ballet class and a fugitive from the law—dressed in a sequined tiger suit.

Seven

Charlie peered cautiously around. She didn't hear any store alarms or see any police with hound dogs hunting for her. The shoppers in the mall were going about their business, paying no attention to her. Apparently the tiger pantsuit, though ugly and too big, was less conspicuous than the baby-blue leotard.

She tried to figure out where Emma and Lindsey would have gone to. She could eliminate Nevins from her search since she knew they'd already been there. She also knew they weren't eating somewhere, since they'd just had hot dogs.

The next big store closest to Nevins was Horner's. It was the most logical place to look. Rolling up the pant legs and cuffs of her droopy outfit, Charlie headed toward the large department store.

She walked through the automatic sliding glass doors into the busy store. Horner's was set up with mirrors everywhere so that it sometimes looked like there were aisles where there weren't. If you weren't paying attention you could wind up smacking right into your own reflection.

Charlie walked up and down every aisle. She tried not to be distracted but occasionally she'd stop to examine a case of brightly colored watches or to try on a pair of sunglasses. Then she'd scold herself for wasting time and move on.

Frustrated and tired, Charlie stopped a moment to get her bearings. She looked up the aisle, and what she saw made her panic. A security guard in a navy-blue uniform was heading straight for her. Maybe he'd been alerted to look for the pantsuit thief.

She wasn't sure if he'd spotted her or not, but she quickly ducked down behind the nearest rack of men's sports coats and waited for him to pass.

The guard stopped right in front of the coats and looked around. He was young; Charlie guessed he was only about nineteen or twenty. He had short blond hair, steely blue eyes, and wore a look of serious determination.

Charlie ducked down even lower as the guard was joined by another security guard, a tall, thin black woman with a walkie-talkie in her hand. "How's it going today, Daryl?" the woman addressed the other guard pleasantly.

"Very well, thanks, Johnson," Daryl answered, all business. "I've already nabbed two teenage shoplifters this morning."

"You're really on a roll there, Daryl," the woman commented, with just a hint of laughter in her voice. "Looks like you're trying for the Security Guard of the Month Award. How many collars have you made this week?"

"Exactly fifteen," Daryl answered proudly. "These kids think they can shoplift with impunity. Well, those days are over, let me tell you. I'm going to watch every kid in this store like a hawk."

Daryl walked off briskly. The woman looked after

him, smiled, and shook her head, and then walked off in the opposite direction.

Charlie breathed for what seemed like the first time since she'd seen the guard coming toward her. Just her luck, she was wandering around in a stolen outfit in a store that had a maniac security guard.

When she was sure Daryl was gone, she crept out from behind the coats and made her way to the up escalator. She let it carry her along, not exactly sure where she should look next. She wasn't really sure why she was bothering. She'd just about given up on ever finding Emma and Lindsey.

She got off the escalator on the second floor—and there they were! Emma and Lindsey were standing at the Madame Lacroix makeup counter, dabbing their fingers in the pots of eyeshadow powder and streaking them onto their lids.

Charlie didn't know how to approach them. She was afraid they'd run away when they saw her. She decided it was best to act casual.

"Hi, you guys," she said breezily, as if she'd just happened to run into them. Emma and Lindsey whirled around and faced her with trapped, guilty expressions on their faces.

"What are you doing here?" Emma asked. "You're supposed to be in ballet class."

"*I'm* supposed to be in ballet class?" Charlie shrieked. Then, not wanting to make a scene, she lowered her voice to a whisper. "What about the two of you? You're supposed to be in ballet class, too."

"That's our business," Emma said huffily.

"How'd you get out?" Lindsey asked.

Charlie told them the story of the mouse. ". . . and

63

then when everyone was running around screaming, I just ducked out," she concluded.

"Neat," Emma said, admiring Charlie's quick thinking. "Maybe you're not as big a twerp as I thought you were."

"Thanks loads," Charlie snapped.

"I can't say I love your outfit, though," Emma added. "Did you just buy it?"

"How could I buy anything?" Charlie demanded. "My wallet, my clothes, everything's back at Miss Claudine's."

"Then how'd you wind up in that weird getup?" Lindsey wanted to know.

Charlie told them *that* story. "What a riot," Emma said, laughing. "At least you saved poor Janine from getting that ugly thing for a present."

"I guess I'll mail it back to the boutique or something," Charlie said. "It's a little better than walking around in a leotard."

"Not much," said Emma, wrinkling up her nose as she looked at the outfit.

"You've really been busy," Lindsey commented, impressed with Charlie's adventures. "We've just been wandering around, looking at things and trying stuff on."

"I can see that," said Charlie, studying their makeup-smeared faces. Emma was now wearing five different-colored stripes of eye makeup. Her cheeks were smudged with three stripes of badly blended blush, and she had silver sparkly powder all over her forehead.

The makeup looked even more strange on Lindsey. The entire area under one eyebrow was completely green, the other eye area was covered in bright blue. She wore a purplish lipstick on her top lip and a reddish-brown color on the bottom.

"It's good that you're here," Emma said cheerfully. "We've run out of face space for trying on makeup. You're a completely unused face, like a blank piece of paper to draw on."

Charlie didn't know what to say. She didn't want to wind up looking like Emma and Lindsey. Still, she was surprised to discover how glad she was that they were finally being nice to her. Now that they were all in trouble together, it seemed as if they were united by a special bond. And after everything she'd just been through, it felt good to have friendly faces around her.

"Come on over here," Emma said, taking Charlie by the arm. "Madame Lacroix is really for old ladies. They don't have any good colors." She pulled Charlie over to a counter with a sign that said Dazzlers.

"Besides," Lindsey said to Charlie in a confidential tone, "we have to keep moving from counter to counter before the salesladies yell at us. They don't really like you using the samples once they figure out that you're not going to buy anything."

Emma stood Charlie in front of the mirror on the counter. "You have sort of hazel eyes, so I think we'll start with some green eyeshadow," she said, picking up a thick crayonlike stick of green makeup with gold flecks running through it. "Now close your eyes."

Charlie let Emma draw lines in the creases of her lids and then smudge them with strong, confident fingers. "Wow," she said when she opened her eyes and looked in the mirror. "It looks kind of good."

"You need mascara and a highlight color," Emma commented, studying her face.

"How did you get so good at this?" Charlie asked as Emma smeared a gold creamy shadow under her eyebrows.

"I'm going to be an artist when I'm older," Emma explained matter-of-factly. "Putting on makeup is just like painting, only you do it on a face instead of on paper. It's really just color and shadow and highlights. I learned all about that stuff when I took painting classes after school last year."

"I couldn't do it," said Lindsey, leaning up against the counter and watching Emma work on Charlie's face. "I'm not sure what I want to be when I'm older. I learned to ski last winter, and I thought about being an Olympic skier. But that's not really a job."

"You could be a ski instructor," Charlie suggested, studying her made-up eyes in the mirror.

"Maybe," agreed Lindsey thoughtfully. "What do you want to be?"

"I'm not totally sure," Charlie said as Emma blended a pink cream blush into her cheeks. "I just know I want to be on TV. I guess that means I want to be an actress. But maybe I could be a TV newsperson, or a game-show host. I don't really care, just as long as it has to do with TV."

"I'll tell you what I don't want to be," said Emma. "I don't want to be a ballerina."

"That's for sure," agreed Lindsey. "What kind of stuff did they do after we left?"

"We did something to do with Arabs," Charlie told her. "You had to stand on one foot. It was dumb."

"Do you mean arabesques?" Emma asked.

"I think so," Charlie said. "I guess you already know all this stuff."

"Some of it," Emma muttered. "You need some lipstick," she added, surveying the different colors that were set out in little sample pots. "I think a goldish color would be good for you."

"What gets me," said Lindsey, "is that everybody else already knows the stuff. Miss Claudine just expected us to know it, too. How can we know it if no one explains it to us?"

"You do sort of pick it up," Emma said, dabbing one color onto Charlie's lips and then rubbing it off. "Too orange," she decided. "And Miss Claudine would eventually come around and start twisting your body into the right positions. Somehow you just get the hang of it."

"Were you good at ballet?" Charlie managed to mumble while Emma applied another color lipstick.

"Naw," Emma admitted. "I stank. My last teacher said I wasn't trying. She was right, I wasn't."

"I think I would stink even if I tried," said Charlie. "I was trying to do the Arab thing and I stank. I'm terrible at anything that has to do with moving around. Moving is my worst thing."

"That's all in your head," Lindsey argued. "Nobody's bad at moving."

"I am," Charlie insisted. "You'd probably be good at it, since you're athletic."

"No way," said Lindsey, as if the suggestion that she might be good at ballet were an insult. "Ballet is totally different, it's so . . . so frilly."

"You do have a fabulous port de bras," Emma teased mischievously.

Lindsey quickly crossed her arms defensively. Charlie and Emma looked at her scowling face and started to giggle. Getting the joke, Lindsey's frown slowly cracked into a smile, and she joined their laughter.

Charlie was the first to stop laughing. She'd spotted Daryl, the security guard, heading their way. This time there was no mistake. His steely eyes were staring right at them.

"We'd better get out of here," said Charlie, nodding toward the approaching guard.

"We're not doing anything," Emma protested.

"That guy hates kids," Charlie said quickly. "He'll call our parents even if we're innocent. Besides, I'm wearing this sort-of-stolen clothing."

"You'd better tuck in those tags," Emma said, eyeing the two tags hanging from Charlie's wrists. "They're sort of a giveaway, don't you think?"

"Shoot," whispered Charlie, frantically stuffing the tags up her sleeve.

"Hey, you kids," the guard shouted. "Stop where you are!"

The girls froze for a second, then, without further discussion they turned and raced down the aisle.

"Stop!" called the guard, running after them.

"Maybe we *should* stop," said Charlie as they careened around the side of a scarf counter.

"Forget it," panted Emma. "Do you want your mother to have to come down and pick you up at the security office?"

"I thought you didn't care about getting into trouble," Lindsey reminded Emma.

Emma shot Lindsey an annoyed look. "Just be quiet and keep running!" she ordered. "He's getting closer!"

Eight

Charlie, Emma, and Lindsey crouched low as they hurried along the scarf counter. They'd given the security guard the slip—for the moment. He stood in the aisle, looking for them.

"Now what?" Lindsey turned to Emma and demanded.

"How should I know?" Emma hissed back as she ventured a peek over the top of the counter.

"Keep your head down," Charlie snapped. "He'll see you."

"Well, we can't stay *here* forever," Emma reminded her needlessly. "I have to see if the coast is clear, don't I?"

The security guard was now standing absolutely still, like a wild animal sniffing the air for the scent of its prey. His blue eyes narrowed as he surveyed the rows of merchandise, looking for anything unusual.

"That guy gives me the creeps," commented Charlie fearfully.

"Yeah," Lindsey agreed. "He has this never-give-up quality. I can imagine him still looking for us when we're seventy-five."

"Shhhh," Emma shushed them. "He will be if you two keep blabbing."

At that moment the guard seemed to sense their presence and headed down the aisle toward them.

"Let's go," whispered Lindsey. The three girls kept low and scooted across the aisle.

"I said stop," yelled the guard, catching sight of them. "Stop this minute!"

In seconds the girls were running pell-mell down the aisle, weaving paths through the shoppers. Daryl broke into a run and was quickly right behind them.

The girls' hearts raced. They knew it was only a matter of seconds before he nabbed one of them. Yet they seemed to be getting away.

A quick check over her shoulder told Charlie what had happened. Two teenage boys wearing gray Horner's stockroom jackets had wheeled a long rack full of fur coats across the aisle, blocking the guard's path. One boy had stopped to tie his shoelace. "Move that thing!" Charlie heard the guard shout.

"Hold your horses," the boy snapped back.

Charlie knew this was their lucky break, but they had to act fast. "I don't think we can outrun him," Charlie said, breathing hard. "Let's find someplace to hide."

The girls quickly ducked behind a rack of ladies' nightgowns in the lingerie department. "There's a dressing room over there," Emma told Charlie and Lindsey. Unable to come up with a better plan, Charlie and Lindsey followed as Emma scrambled toward the ladies' dressing room.

"Grab something so you look like you're trying it on," Emma instructed them.

"Like what?" asked Lindsey, looking around at the rows of fancy, lacy ladies' lingerie.

"Like anything," Emma said, quickly handing Lind-

70

sey a frilly slip, and Charlie a bra on a plastic hanger. She took a purple flowered nightgown for herself. "Just get into that dressing room."

The woman at the entrance of the dressing room eyed them suspiciously, but gave them each a ticket marked One Item. "I don't think that will fit you," she said, looking at the black, underwired, lace bra Charlie carried in her hand. "I doubt you're a C-cup."

"Oh, you'd be surprised," Charlie said coolly, a little shocked by her own boldness.

The woman rolled her eyes and shook her head wearily, but let her pass. Once inside the dressing room, the girls made their way down the single long, narrow aisle lined with individual stalls. They looked at the feet under the louvered stall doors until they found one stall at the very end that was empty.

"Now what do we do?" Lindsey asked.

"Stop asking that," Emma snapped.

"For someone who said she doesn't care about getting in trouble, you sure seem nervous," Lindsey challenged.

"I meant I don't care about getting into trouble with my mother, or the principal, or like that. I've never been in trouble with the police before."

"He isn't really a policeman," said Charlie. "He's just a store guard."

"Close enough for me," Emma said, leaning against the wall. "The only thing to do now is wait in here and hope we've lost him."

The girls slid down the wall of the dressing room and sat in a row on the floor, opposite the full-length mirror on the wall.

They sat in silence for several minutes, staring at their

reflections. "You know, we do look pretty weird," Lindsey said finally. "How come I have a different-colored eyeshadow on each eye?"

"Because the saleslady in the makeup department chased us away from the counter before I could finish making up your other eye, remember?" Emma reminded her.

"Oh, yeah," Lindsey recalled. "Charlie doesn't look too bad. Her makeup looks nice."

"But you're not wearing this stupid outfit," Charlie said.

"Why don't you take it off," Lindsey suggested. "It makes you kind of easy to spot."

"I have to return it somehow," Charlie explained. "Besides, we'd stand out anyway with all this makeup on and with the two of us in matching blue tights."

"I can't believe you told that woman you could fit into that bra," Emma giggled.

Charlie laughed at the memory. "What else was I supposed to say? You're the one who handed it to me." She held the bra up in front of her. "It's strange to think that someday maybe I *will* fit into this."

"I can't picture myself with a woman's body, can you?" asked Lindsey seriously.

"I definitely can," Emma answered. "I want to be nice and slim."

Charlie got to her feet and took the bra off the hanger. She wiggled her arms out of the sleeves of the tiger top and put the bra on over her leotard. Then she slipped her arms back in and stood with her hands on her hips in front of Emma and Lindsey. The stiff underwiring of the bra gave her a full shape. "This is what I'll probably look like," she giggled.

Emma and Lindsey broke into gales of laughter at the ridiculous sight. "You're *too* strange," panted Emma with a note of admiration in her voice. Lindsey was too convulsed with laughter to say anything.

Suddenly, Emma held up her hand for quiet. "Shhhh, listen," she ordered them sharply.

Sure enough, they heard the unmistakable sound of the security guard's voice, though they couldn't quite hear what was being said. Emma slowly cracked the stall door open a half-inch, and the girls crowded together, trying to make out the guard's words.

"I just came on duty and I don't know who's in there," they heard the woman at the door tell the guard. From the sound of her voice they could tell that she wasn't the same woman who'd let them in. "You can't go in there," the woman insisted.

"Either you check for me or I'm going in," the guard insisted.

Lindsey looked at Charlie with a horrified expression. "It'd be easier to escape a pack of bloodhounds."

"I can't go in until I get someone to relieve me at the door here," the woman argued.

"We have to get out of here, right now," Emma said.

"But he's standing right in front of us," Lindsey pointed out. "Face it, we're goners. We're trapped in here."

They could tell from the tone of his voice that the guard was angry with the woman at the door. They were arguing in low tones, then the guard raised his voice. "All right," he snapped, "I'll be back with a saleswoman to check the dressing room."

Without further discussion the girls slipped out of the stall and made their way toward the front of the narrow dressing room with their backs pressed flat against the stall doors.

Near the inside of the door they huddled together. The woman at the entrance was sitting on a high stool, leafing through the pages of a magazine. They exchanged worried glances, and then Lindsey dropped to her hands and knees and began crawling silently out the door. Emma and Charlie got onto their knees, as well.

Emma and Charlie watched as Lindsey made it safely around the corner of the partition separating the entrance of the dressing room from the rest of the store. The woman never looked up from her magazine. Emma scrambled out next. She, too, rounded the partition safely.

Charlie sucked in her breath and began crawling with her head down. She didn't dare to breathe or even look up at the woman. She just crawled and crawled—and suddenly stopped right under the woman's feet! She couldn't go any farther; her pant leg was caught on a carpet staple that was sticking up from the floor.

With trembling hands, Charlie reached back and worked the cloth free from the staple. Some instinct made her look up quickly, and her eyes met those of the saleslady which were boring down at her.

Charlie jumped to her feet and faced the woman. Before either of them could speak, the guard approached with the saleswoman who'd originally let them into the dressing room.

"There's one of them now," yelled the guard, catching sight of Charlie.

"And she's stealing a bra!" added the saleswoman with the guard. "She didn't have that chest when she came in."

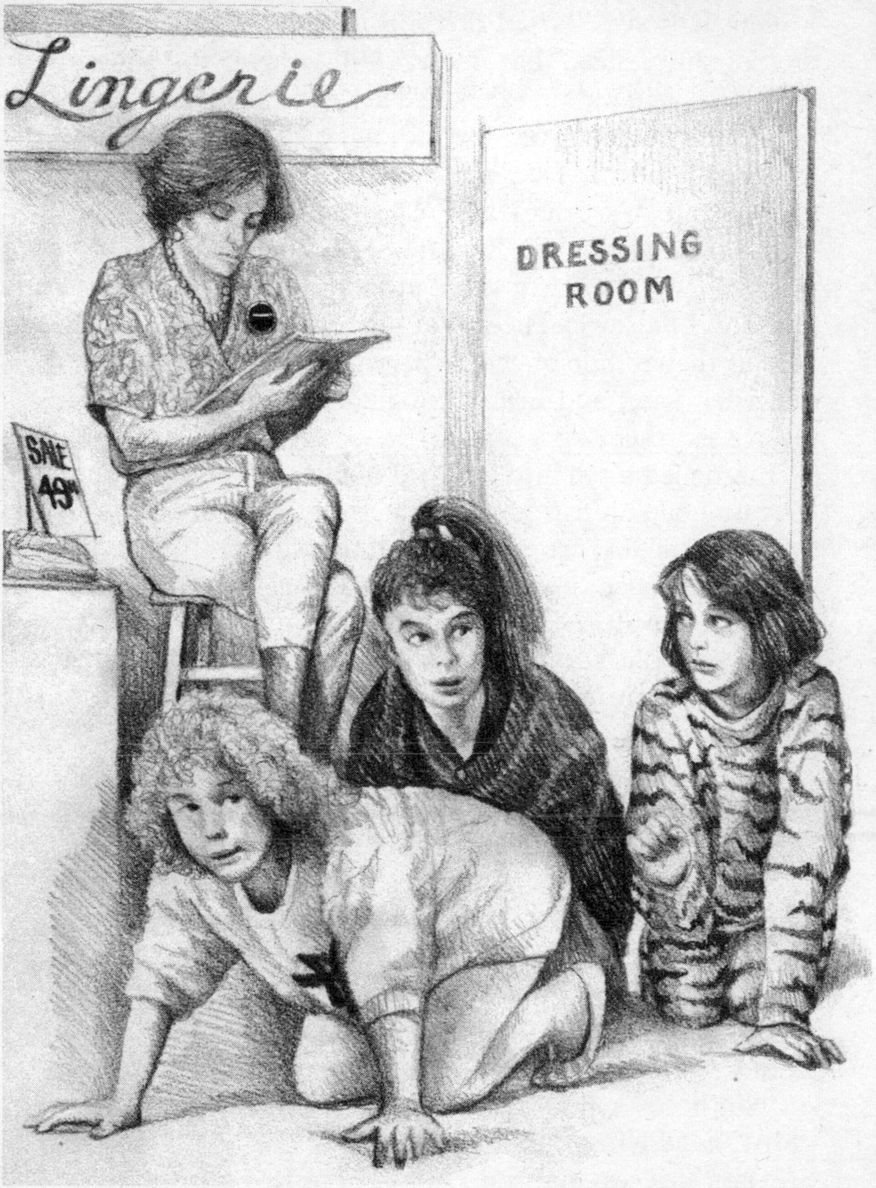
Lingerie
DRESSING
ROOM

Charlie's eyes darted down to her chest, and to her horror she realized that she was still wearing the underwire bra she'd put on as a joke back in the dressing stall.

The saleswoman at the doorway reached out and grabbed her arm. That was enough to snap Charlie out of her state of frozen terror. She yanked her arm away and darted across the lingerie department.

"This way," came a voice at her side. It was Emma. She and Lindsey had been waiting for Charlie, crouched low at the far side of the hosiery counter. Charlie took off with them, and heard the guard yelling "Stop!" as he chased them once again.

Emma led them into a crowd of people waiting at the elevator bank. Just as they got there, a door opened. "Excuse me, excuse me," they mumbled as they wriggled and pushed their way to the front of the crowd and onto the elevator. They ran directly to the back wall of the elevator car and flattened themselves against the wall as the throng of shoppers packed in in front of them.

The security guard screeched to a stop in front of the elevator door as it began to close. Looking over heads and under legs he searched for them. They weren't sure if he saw them or not, but in seconds the door closed and they were on their way to the upper floors of the store.

Charlie leaned back against the wall with her eyes shut, panting. "This is like a nightmare," she whispered.

"Shhhhh," whispered Emma. "We'll get off at the third floor. I have an idea."

The third was the top floor. There was a restaurant

and a rest room just outside the elevator. The girls headed for the ladies' room.

"Thanks for waiting," Charlie said as she plopped down on a chair in the front powder room.

"No problem," Lindsey assured her. "We're in this mess together." She looked at Charlie and added, "I think you'd better take that thing off."

"Oh, this stupid thing," Charlie muttered as she wiggled out of the bra. "I keep getting accused of stealing all this stuff I don't even want!"

"Listen, this is my plan," said Emma. "We find the fire stairs and take them down to the bottom floor. We've just got to get out of this store."

"Good idea," Lindsey agreed. "Let's go."

Trying to look calm and casual, the girls walked out of the ladies' room. Charlie hung the bra on the arm of the first mannequin she saw.

They followed the walls until they came to a sign marked Fire Exit—Use in Emergency Only. They ducked into the stairwell and made their way down the three flights of stairs.

They stopped on the first floor. "Just act cool and head straight for the first exit you see," Emma instructed them. "Once we're back out in the mall we'll head as far away from Horner's as we can get."

"That will bring us right back to Miss Claudine's," Lindsey objected.

"Don't worry about that now," Emma said. "Let's just get out of here."

Charlie cracked open the door and looked around. "The nearest doorway is right through the pet department on the left," she reported. "Follow me."

The girls headed for the pet department. They

stepped through the archway that led them into the aisles full of adorable kittens and puppies. The door into the mall was just yards away, right past the large cages full of tiny yellow canaries.

"Almost there," Lindsey whispered under her breath encouragingly.

Suddenly an all-too-familiar voice resounded in their ears. "Stop those kids!" It was the guard racing toward them from the other end of the first floor.

"Go!" yelled Lindsey.

Nine

The door was so near, but Daryl, the security guard, was closing in on them with lightning speed. Lindsey bounded out the door, Emma was right behind her. Charlie would have been third if the cuff of her pants hadn't picked that moment to come unrolled and trip her up.

"Darn!" she cried as she reached out for something to break her fall. Her fingers clutched the strong gold wires of the large canary cage and she brought it crashing down to the ground as she fell.

The air was immediately full of chirping yellow birds. The impact of the fall had sprung the catch of the cage door, freeing the canaries.

"Young lady!" cried a salesman, running out from behind the counter. "Look what you've done!"

Charlie looked up at him with frightened eyes. How was she going to explain to her mother that even though she'd run away from ballet class, stolen a pantsuit and a bra, and freed all the canaries in the pet department—none of it was her fault? She'd have to think of something, because this certainly had to be the end of the line for her.

But just as the salesman was about to grab her, he collided with the guard who was running toward her from the opposite direction. They hit with a slam, bouncing off one another into the rabbit cages on one side, and the snake tanks on the other.

Charlie saw her opportunity and took it. In a split second she was up and out the door. This time there was no sign of Emma and Lindsey.

Charlie turned sharply to her left and kept running. A sharp *pssst* sound made her stop and look around. "Over here!" It was Lindsey waving to her from the long, covered entrance of a men's clothing store. Long glass showcases with mannequins in suits shielded them on either side.

"I can't believe you got away again," said Emma, joining them in the hallway formed by the two showcases.

"Me, neither," Charlie agreed. "Now, what do we do?"

The girls scanned the mall in front of them. Sure enough, Daryl was heading toward them, looking furious. Besides the stores, the only other thing near them was a small trailer with a low wooden stage in front of it. A sign read: Eastbridge Mall Annual Talent Contest at 12:30 P.M. People were already starting to sit on the metal folding chairs that were set up in front of the stage.

Reading the sign made Charlie suddenly think about time. "Gosh, what time is it?" she asked.

Emma and Lindsey shrugged. "Wait a minute, I think there's a clock inside this store," Lindsey said, holding her hands up to her eyes and peering through the glass door into the men's store. "It's twelve-fifteen," she reported.

"Listen, I have a plan," said Emma seriously. "I say

we walk casually over to that talent show and mingle with the crowd. Then we make our way to the side of the trailer and, when the coast is clear, we run out to the parking lot and wait for Charlie's mother."

"But all our clothes are back at Miss Claudine's," Lindsey objected.

Emma thought for a moment. "I don't know, say that you forgot them. I can't think of everything!"

"We'll say Miss Claudine is such a nut that she locked us out without our clothes," Charlie suggested. "We'll tell her that only Emma was able to grab her things before Miss Claudine went on a wild rampage and threw everyone out of the studio. My mother won't let us go back if she thinks Miss Claudine is a total nut case."

"Brilliant," said Emma. "I really misjudged you, Charlie. I thought you were just a goody-goody."

"Well, you're not as weird as I thought," said Charlie.

"What about me?" asked Lindsey. "What did you guys think of me?"

"Jock," Emma and Charlie answered at once.

"Is that bad?" asked Lindsey, bewildered. "I *am* a jock."

"Sometimes it's annoying," Charlie said, "but you're an okay jock."

"Yeah," Emma agreed, "you're not the bossy, loud-mouthed kind. If I had to be on a team, I'd be on yours."

Lindsey smiled at them. "Thanks. You guys are okay, too."

The three girls smiled at one another, then Emma grew serious. "It's good we all like each other because we might end up as cellmates in jail if that guard finds us. There's a pretty good crowd over there. Let's get over there."

They peeked around the corner of the glass showcase. Daryl had walked past them and was at the end of the mall corridor. It looked like he was about to circle back up their way.

"Keep your head down and walk slowly," Emma instructed as they headed across the corridor.

Wordlessly, the girls made their way through the crowd and headed toward the trailer. The guard was now standing right in front of the metal chairs looking all around.

Just as they were about to slip past the trailer, a woman with curly white hair popped her head out of its side door and called to them. "Hurry, girls," she called, "the dog act ahead of you hasn't shown up. I need you to go on first."

The girls looked at one another. The woman had obviously mistaken them for someone else. "We're not— " Lindsey began to explain, but a quick poke from Emma stopped her. The guard was walking up the center aisle between the chairs. He hadn't seen them, but in a minute he would.

"No problem," said Charlie as the girls quickly stepped up into the trailer. Inside, the place was crowded with people, most of them teenagers and kids, practicing their acts. There was a small boy with a wooden dummy on his lap, a teenage girl with an accordion, two small twin girls in tuxedoes and tap shoes, a rap group dressed in red nylon jackets, a tall, thin boy with a guitar, and assorted other people either dressing or rehearsing their acts.

A girl of about twelve who was holding a flute came over to them. "You must be the Tip Toe Dancers," she said, looking them over icily. "I heard you were the act to beat, but you don't look so hot to me."

"Then you obviously don't see too well," Charlie hissed back. "We're the greatest."

"Hmmmph," the girl said, turning on her heels and storming away.

"This is just terrific!" whispered Lindsey. "Every time we turn around we're in an even bigger mess than we were before!"

"Would you rather go out there and get caught?" asked Emma, hands on hips.

"We'd better come up with an act," Charlie reminded them. "The Tip Toe Dancers are now on first. I can see why the woman thought we were in the show. We have all this makeup on and everything."

"Take off that tiger suit," said Emma, taking off her own jacket. "I still have my leotard on under my clothes. At least we'll all have matching costumes. Lindsey, you take off your T-shirt."

"No way," Lindsey argued.

"Lindsey, this is an emergency," Charlie coaxed as she pulled the tiger top over her head. "You look fine in the leotard. Honestly, you do."

"Oh, all right," Lindsey agreed, pulling the shirt over her head sullenly. In a minute the girls stood in their blue leotards, clutching their clothes.

"What are we going to do once we get on stage?" asked Lindsey.

"Dance on our tiptoes, I guess," Emma said with a shrug of her shoulders. "I wonder what happened to the real Tip Toe Dancers."

"It's showtime, ladies," said the white-haired woman, ushering the three girls to the main trailer door which led out onto the wooden stage. "Mr. Johnson on stage has the tape you sent all set to go."

"G-g-great," Charlie stammered, smiling feebly at the woman.

The girls stood in the door just as a man onstage announced to the audience, "Please welcome our first act, the Tip Toe Dancers."

There was a polite ripple of applause. The girls stood stock still in the doorway, still holding their clothing, frozen with stage fright. "Come on, girls," the woman encouraged, giving each of them a gentle push onto the stage, "give them your best."

Dropping their clothing in a pile at the side of the stage, the girls stood and listened to the music. Charlie recognized it as a piece from *The Nutcracker,* a ballet that her mother sometimes liked to play on the stereo.

Charlie knew they couldn't just stand there. *Pretend you're on TV,* she told herself, and began doing an arabesque, just as she'd learned in Miss Claudine's. To her surprise, she was able to keep her balance.

Emma knew the move from her previous classes and imitated Charlie. Lindsey did the same. With their legs extended behind them, the three girls began hopping in a circle around the stage.

Emma then leaped out of the circle and began spinning around the stage with her arms over her head. Lindsey and Charlie did the same. They were surprised at how the music carried them along. Soon they were leaping across the stage and kicking their legs out in front, throwing their arms wide to either side. The

music was so lively, it just naturally lent itself to jumping around joyfully.

Occasionally they'd smack into one another, but they'd just go right on dancing. The audience seemed to assume that they were a comedy act, and laughed and clapped along with them.

Every so often they'd glance out front. Daryl, the guard, was standing in front, but he wasn't paying any attention to them, even as they danced right before his very eyes. He was looking for three girls who were dressed differently and who most certainly were not performing in a talent contest—or so he thought.

"I wish he'd go away," Charlie whispered to Emma as she twirled past her.

"Just keep dancing," Emma muttered back, smiling at the audience as she spun by.

As Charlie turned around she noticed three girls just about their age standing in the trailer doorway wearing gauzy pink tutus and angry expressions. They were clearly the real Tip Toe Dancers.

Charlie and Lindsey looked at Emma with wide, panicked eyes. Emma just kept smiling at the audience, leaping and twirling. She took their hands and danced them into a circle.

They turned out from their circle just in time to see the guard shrug his shoulders and walk away slowly—a defeated man.

Not wasting a second, Emma danced over to the pile of clothing and scooped up her things gracefully. Charlie and Lindsey did the same. Emma then danced down the wooden stairs at the center of the stage with Charlie and Lindsey right behind her.

The audience laughed and clapped as they twirled the rest of the way out into the mall.

Ten

Charlie, Emma, and Lindsey stopped twirling and broke into a run. They weren't sure which way they were headed. All they knew was this was their chance to get far away from that side of the mall.

When Charlie ran past the boutique where she'd tried on the tiger suit, she kept her head down. Then, summoning her courage she ran back to the store, threw the outfit in the door and raced after Emma and Lindsey. It felt great to be free at last of the ugly "stolen" outfit.

The three girls ran down the ramp to the lower level and, before they knew it, they were in the corridor that led to Miss Claudine's. "We made it," panted Lindsey.

Oddly enough Charlie and Emma knew what she meant. Miss Claudine's did seem like a friendly place somehow. Certainly no one had chased them—and Miss Claudine had actually been pretty nice to them.

They stood in front of Miss Claudine's and looked at one another. Emma peeked in the glass of the front door. She could see into half the studio. "This must be the 'ballet culture' part. It looks like they're all just sitting around on the floor, and Miss Claudine is telling them something," she reported. "What do you think we should do?"

"I'm tired of running and making up stories," Charlie said. "I just want to go inside and finish up the class. If she tells my mother, then she does. I don't even care anymore."

"Me, too," said Lindsey. "At least we're not sitting in some store security office or anything."

"Okay," agreed Emma skeptically. "Let's go."

They opened the front door as quietly as they could. Immediately they heard the pleasant sound of Miss Claudine's voice. ". . . and so, *chéries,* though much of *Swan Lake* is very sad, in the end, the evil Rothbart's spell is broken, and Prince Siegfried and his beloved swan princess are united in the kingdom under the sea—together at last."

One by one, Charlie, then Emma, then Lindsey slipped into the studio and sat at the back of the group of girls. This time Miss Claudine clearly saw them, but she didn't say anything. She simply continued with what she was saying. "The end of this ballet is so beautiful that the entire audience weeps. The swans lie gracefully on the stage as we see Siegfried and Odette sail off in a magical boat." Miss Claudine's blue eyes seemed to mist up at the very memory of the scene.

Charlie, Emma, and Lindsey looked at the faces of the other girls. They, too, seemed moved by the story. It made them wish they'd been there to hear the whole thing.

"*Swan Lake* has some of the most beautiful chorus work ever seen," Miss Claudine continued. "The dancers must move together as if they were almost one body. It's fine to be a star on your own, but before you can be that, you must be able to work as part of a group."

The girls weren't sure, but they suspected that Miss

Claudine was directing the next thing she said at them. "That is why I never force a student. Each student must be moved by the music and her own inner spirit. Either you choose companionship with other dancers and a love for ballet, or you do not."

Charlie wasn't sure about her love for ballet, yet when she'd been dancing on the stage, as goofy as it had looked, she had been swept up by the music. She'd felt free and happy.

Emma drew imaginary circles on the wood floor as Miss Claudine continued to talk about the love of ballet. It struck her that Miss Claudine really believed what she was saying. Being near someone so passionate about the subject sort of changed her attitude about ballet.

Lindsey, too, was struck by Miss Claudine in a new way. She loved teamwork. She'd never realized there was so much of it involved with ballet.

"Go now, *mesdemoiselles,*" said Miss Claudine. "Hold the image of yourselves as beautiful swans in your heads until I see you all again on Wednesday. *Au revoir.*"

Charlie, Emma, and Lindsey jumped up and ran for the dressing room, relieved that Miss Claudine hadn't scolded them. They put on their clothes and washed the makeup off their faces in the bathroom.

"It's like she doesn't care whether we're here or not," commented Emma, sounding almost hurt. "I don't even know if she knew we were gone."

"She knew," Lindsey said. "I guess it's like she said, she doesn't force anybody to do anything."

"That's almost unnatural coming from an adult," Charlie commented.

"I'll say," Emma agreed.

"It's like being treated like an adult," Lindsey said. The girls thought about that for a minute. It was strange and unfamiliar, but they liked the idea.

As the three of them headed for the door, older students were coming in. There were boys as well as girls in this class. They looked graceful and confident to the younger girls.

A few moments later, the three friends stood in front of Miss Claudine's waiting for Charlie's mother to pick them up. "Will you guys be going on Wednesday?" Charlie asked.

"I don't know," answered Emma. "You going?"

"I'll probably have to," Charlie answered.

"It's not really that bad," Lindsey said. "Besides, we have one another for company."

Slowly a smile spread across each girl's face. "It's true," said Charlie, "we do have one another."

The girls each looked from one to the next and started to laugh. The whole morning's events suddenly seemed very funny.

"You girls certainly seem to have had a good time," said Mrs. Clark happily as she approached them. "I told you you'd like ballet. What did you do on your first day?"

"Ummm, not much," Charlie answered with a mischievous smile. "We all just sort of got to know one another."

Don't miss NO WAY BALLET #2
A Twist of Fate by Suzanne Weyn